Origins of Desire in Orchid Fens

This is a work of fiction. All characters, organizations, and events
portrayed in this novella are either products of the author's imagination
or are reproduced as fiction. No part of this book may be used or reproduced in
any manner for the purpose of training artificial intelligence technologies
or systems.

Origins of Desire in Orchid Fens

Cover art by Jay Rasgorshek
https://jayrasgorshek.com

Edited by Selena Middleton

Published by Stelliform Press
Hamilton, Ontario, Canada
https://stelliform.press

Printed on 100% recycled paper

Library and Archives Canada Cataloguing in Publication
Title: Origins of desire in orchid fens / Lynn Hutchinson Lee.
Names: Hutchinson Lee, Lynn, author.
Identifiers: Canadiana (print) 20240476514 | Canadiana (ebook) 20240476530
| ISBN 9781738316519 (softcover) | ISBN 9781738316526 (EPUB)
Subjects: LCGFT: Novellas.
Classification: LCC PS8615.U835 O75 2025 | DDC C813/.6—dc23

For my mother Grace, who found orchids in the Horseshoe Lake marsh
For my daughters Zoe and Riel, who played there

Origins of Desire in Orchid Fens

LYNN HUTCHINSON LEE

Stelliform Press
Hamilton, Ontario

A Partial Morphology of the Orchid
(Partialis morphologiam lacus)

The orchid arranges her flower in the image of the pollinator she desires, whether bee, wasp, moth or fly (Smaller 1997, 198).

The petals — fleshy, succulent, x-rated — can be rolled in, bruised, or caressed. They flare, enfold, embrace; the perfume — heady, vanilla-ish, cinnamon-ish — draws you in.
     The lip opens.
     "The pollinator, in the belief that the bloom is a longed-for lover, enters the flower" (Peele et al. 1923, 237).

Upon discovering that the orchid is merely an orchid and not a lover, the disappointed insect departs, bathed in the orchid's pollen (Hallow 1957, 156).

The insect then flies in search of a new lover, and, constantly drawn in and disillusioned, inadvertently spreads pollen throughout the orchid population.
     Up to several hundred orchids may be visited, with the hopes of the insect being continually dashed (Lake 2021, 79).

References

Smaller, Lavinia. 1997. *Origins of Desire in Northern Orchid Fens.* Jansons, Fugler & Smith.
Peele, Simon et al. 1923. *The Orchid as Lover.* Cockburn & Farrow.
Hallow, E.D. 1957. "Longing and Disappointment." *Orchidaceae Botanica* 10(7): 148-170.
Lake, Ro-Anne. 2021. *The Reproduction of Despair and Hope.* Fairchild, Wessex & Fontaine.

Between Places

If you zoom in, we're here on the map, a small red teardrop side-ways from Sudbury and a bit north, between a shifting, humming marsh, and Nurses Creek, a small haunted river. The marsh lies more or less to the east of our town, the river to the west. Although not of the town, together they hold it within their wide embrace.

On the edge of the marsh, nestled in a bay of Orchid Lake, lies the beloved orchid fen, my beating heart; at the other side of town, the narrow river snakes through a dark lace of trees. Nurses Creek — named for Mary-Maud Billings, a young nurse strangled in 1884 by her mining boss lover and thrown into the river — is now stubborn as lime jello, poisoned by defunct mine tailings, and home to the water spirits who honor her memory. The elemental desire of these spirits — dead girls, water girls, the panni raklies — is to drown the men who betrayed or killed them.

Zoom in closer and there's Carminetown; if you switch to earth view you'll see a house, plain, still with its seventy-year-old insulbrick siding. You can't see the two bedrooms, small kitchen, smaller living room. But they're there. Orderly, scoured, impossibly clean, because this is our way.

This is the house where I live with my mother and our secret. The secret that has its hands around my neck. Leaving for work, I pass by the mirror in the hall. The secret tightens its hands, and I make myself small, though I never need reminding. Each day I ask the mirror to forget me. To make me invisible. This is also our way.

When the greenhouse job came up, my mother told me not to take it. *You're not working for them people*, she said. But a greenhouse of heavy-lipped, speckled tropical orchids? How could I say no? I earn a good wage, although I secretly feel money cheapens the purity of the relationship. These tamed orchids — extravagant, startling, lovely — don't weaken me with their beauty. Not like the orchids of my beloved fen.

It was Iris Blythe the Galvestons' housekeeper who hired me, even with my mother's words chasing me like mosquitoes. *Watch out for them gorjos. Remember what that teacher did.*

I kept this new job from her, another secret hidden by telling her I was shelving books at the library, which she has never visited. I go so far as to hide my route to work, circling around behind the mansions on Galveston's road.

Invisible

When I leave our house in the morning, I wear my town face. This face is pale like the endangered lady's slipper of the shore, but underneath lies the hidden stain that can't be washed away. *(Don't tell! Don't let them see who you are!)* The stain was tattooed by my mother, the secret needled into my skin by every barbed word she spoke. Over years, the secret grew, pushed me into its corners, with barely room left for me to breathe. What was Orchid Lovell, other than a secret? I needed to be invisible as air, so people would not only see no stain, but they wouldn't see Orchid Lovell at all.

Didn't my mother call me Orchid because she loves them, a ridiculous name I hated and then grew to love even though it means, more or less, testicle? To be fair, my second name, Rhoda, which I don't mind so much, is well-used among our fowki. So my Mam named me for men's balls. *Thanks Mam. You didn't know, but that's no excuse.*

What's Before Me On My Path

In the morning light slicing through the canopy, the mosquito dance

In the old growth forest, coral root, helleborine, nervous white calypso

In a glade, the lady's slippers where I sit sometimes under the ironwood tree

At the boggy shore, round-leaved orchids, rattlesnake plantain, and the flared pink crests of the open-lipped dragon's mouth

The jewel of the shore, rarest of orchids, and endangered: a single small white lady's slipper

Also at the shore, damselflies — ebony jewelwing, emerald spreadwing, the blue-eyed boreal bluet

Also (always) at the shore: a whispered history of the many beings of the fen as they hunt, feed, dig, hide, wait, love

The Orchid Fen

O the fragrance. O the orchid fen. Knee deep in water and muck, slogging through the marshes and wet fields, the shores of the lake, everything humming, chirping, blurred with mosquito clouds and blackflies. This is why I take the long way to work. Nobody needs to see me. I'm away from the eyes of the town. Who cares that I'm late? Mister Galveston doesn't; my boss has never met me. Puro baro shato, the old big shot has never shown his face around here, not once. He's always off somewhere, checking on his gold mines, meeting, plotting, giving orders, getting drunk at the golf club. A lone shifting shadow without comfort or love: I think that's why he needs the gold.

There is no Missus Galveston. Her name was Louise, and she was birdwatching when she jumped, or fell, or was pushed (depending on who's telling the story) off the Plough River bridge at the far edge of Orchid Lake. I was ten years old when they announced it on the news, and there was a lot of whispering at the time. According to Dalia Doroshenko next door, Louise's head came off and flew to the other side of the river. I asked Dalia how a head could fly across a river, and all she said was *anything can happen where the devil and his dirty work are concerned,* and shooed me away. She later whispered that Louise had left a son, Heron, about my age, a tragic child who drove a nail into his own foot after his mother's body was found. "Then he hid the gash from his dad,"

Dalia said, "till it was nearly too late. When it turned green as Nurses Creek all hell broke loose."

After this, Mister Galveston hired my mother to live in his house where she was to look after Heron; and she left me alone and disconsolate with Dalia. *Heron. Poor sweet little Heron,* my mother said whenever she called. For a time, he was all she could talk about. These days Dalia says Heron is too good looking, a sharp dresser, and when not lending a hand to his father's shady dealings — "You know what I'm talkin about," she says — he parties in Toronto.

Feet still wet from the marsh, I step finally into Galveston's greenhouse and greet the orchids, who don't care about people's lives.

Jack Bachinski: First Sighting

It was about two years ago that I saw him. A Saturday morning, mid-spring, too warm, with snow melting into the waters of the fen. I was at the edge of the marsh with its small shifting islets, their buried roots of grasses and moss in the cold muck. The sun shone through dizzying eddies of snow, and at first I was unsure of what was before me. An islet tilted itself in an unusual way, revealing a body. A man, or maybe not a man. Sometimes, in this place, it's hard to know what's really there or what's a trick played on your eyes.

The shape resembled a man, limbs enmeshed with Labrador Tea and last year's cranberry bushes and cotton grass. The vegetation softening, blurring with the edges of this entangled body. He gathered himself and stood, real as the water, motionless as a deer. His skin wet from the moss, I saw through him. I saw through his long dark hair, through his tissues, his blood vessels, then deeper, to silent pools. *I see you,* I said from somewhere inside myself. In the vision before me, a small boy emerged from this man's hidden self, one hand clutching his mother's, the other his father's. Unsteady steps toward a frog plunging into the water, a dragonfly on a stem. I understand now, looking through this magic lens, that in the core of Jack Bachinski would always live a fen-child. Like me, he and the fen were one.

I moved back behind the trees. I had trespassed on his moment, and felt ashamed; but I also understood it, uniquely his, in the deepest part of my body. I didn't see him again for another year. Or longer. All that time it was only the vision that visited me: a small boy's delight as he ran ahead of his parents. I returned to the waters again and again with a vague hope of seeing him. Of revisiting that strange magic. But it was as if he'd been absorbed by the fen.

Jack Bachinski: Second Sighting

Just after I turned twenty, my mother got sick. A cancer was taking root, and confusion spread throughout her body, brought on by the disease or the painkillers or both. Among other things, she told me to dig up a wild orchid and transplant it into our yard. *Get it from above the fen,* she said, *from that open place near the pines. The far side of the ironwood tree.* She had taught me that a wild orchid needs its own earth and its own air. It cannot be uprooted. When I repeated her own words back to her, she said I knew bugger-all, I was useless, I knew nothing; then she switched her tone and said *pleasepleaseplease* till her desire rose to a chant, chasing me out the door.

It would have been early summer a year ago, not a long time to remember that first meeting. A meeting that enters you like the sky.

My hands were in the loose rich earth, my fingertips feeling for rhizomes. The flower plum-colored, heavy veined pouch, deep cleft. A dark flavor like plum jam or conserve. The imagined taste swelled my tongue.

Too late, I heard quiet footsteps moving over the leaves.

"That's poaching, that is."

I kept my hands around the rhizomes, protecting them from this voice.

"It'll die," said the man standing over me. "You know that, don't you? It'll die and you'll be to blame. Wanna be known as the orchid-killer?" As I crouched, guarding the orchid, he quoted some law at me. A law about harming, harassing, capturing an endangered species.

"A law wouldn't say those things," I said, looking up.

"It sure as hell would," he shot back. I wanted him to go away but now he, too, crouched over the flower. He smelt of the fen, of water lilies and salt. Something caught inside me: I'd seen him before. I knew him. Yes. The man from the islet, arms and legs entwined with the vegetation growing there. I saw the open ease of him. O how beautiful. We looked at each other across the orchid. The moment expanded, filling the air.

"I have to do this for my mother. She's out of her mind."

"Ah," he said, as if he understood.

As we crouched over the dark soil, my heat, shy, went out to meet his, and our two heats met and mingled together. I lifted my hands and the orchid stayed in the earth. We walked back through the fen. He talked about the community of the orchids, never alone, but joined with their sisters and aunts and cousins in an underground net of rhizomes and fungi that fed them. When he fell silent, I asked if there was more. More what, I didn't know. *You want more? There's always more. More* had layers of meanings and possibilities and depths, and I was caught, unsure of any of it. I wanted to climb into this *more* and sink deeper into the freshness of it all. The wonder.

At the road, he held out his hand. "Jack Bachinski, gold miner."

"Fen fanatic, Orchid Lovell."

"No kidding," said Jack Bachinski, suddenly smiling. "Orchid." His tongue, tasting my name in his mouth.

Lies

I can't remember the specific lie I told my mother when I came into her room empty-handed. It was Jack Bachinski's fault that the orchid had not been pulled from the ground.

Where were you? she said.

Just out.

I was calling and you didn't answer.

What's wrong?

Who was that mush?

What mush?

The one I saw you with. He's got all them raklies, them girls, coming and going.

You always do this.

Do what? She latched on to the idea of Jack Bachinski again. *He's too good looking,* she says. *And a gorjo.*

Mother. You're not back in England.

We brought our ways with us, so remember that.

I'm not there. I'm living here in your stupid town. I'm here in your stupid house with you breathing down my neck.

Quit exaggerating, she said, and turned back to the window to watch the moon in the afternoon sky.

Nurses Creek

Over that year I saw Jack Bachinski five or six times, always at the orchid fen. It was our swampy mother — the nest of our complicated humanness, our belonging and desire — that brought us together. And then in spring, a sudden furnace ignited inside me, sent me up in flames. Not the slow sultry heat of the summer fen, but a darker, quicker heat. I didn't need to be a secret with Jack Bachinski. I didn't need to be invisible. I could run at a cliff, any cliff, and leap off.

This is how it feels with Jack.

On this night the dry tailings, hard as stone, are a silvery white like pickerel bellies under the moon. At my instigation we're on a dare, crossing to Nurses Creek where the dead girls swim. Jack knows nothing about the dead girls. The stories about them are only for women. We dance through the mosquitoes toward the edge of the tailings, where the mummified crust stops at Nurses Creek and the current elbows the shore under the birches.

O what a beautiful man is Jack Bachinski. The salt smell of him. I remember, when I first saw him in the fen, thinking he was not one of us, but a green man of the marsh. Even now I'm sometimes confused about this, but I let it slide: tonight he feels fully human.

When Jack isn't with me in the evenings, he goes to the Sylvanite Hotel with the guys. When they get good and drunk, they break into the old work songs, and somebody always starts crying: Frank Turcotte, diagnosed with emphysema from thirty years down the mine; Emile Sorel still crying for his son Dave, crushed ten years ago under a shuttle car. They sing "Bread and Roses." Then they sing "Take This Job and Shove It," and "Which Side Are You On."

Of all the men at the Sylvanite, Jack has the best voice. He sings those songs in my ear while we clutch each other in our slow dance to the river. He sings that he'll bring me a sheet of gold for our future bed, carry it through the forest past the bears. He'll make me a necklace of those little flakes smuggled out of the mine by Mac McCarthy and sold to the men behind the hotel.

Tonight, as we dance, an unearthly sound is in the air, disrupting Jack's voice in my ear. Drifting over from the water, it closes in around us: a high keening like thin wind in the reeds or knives under moonlight, so haunting and beautiful I want to put my hands over my ears, press my head against his chest.

Then, through the mist rising from the river, through the low branches of the trees, I see the water girls: the dreaded panni raklies, drowned, mullered, dead. Here they are before me, skin sliding off their bones, whooping, calling, tearing out from the river, swinging from the birch branches, dancing among the ferns.

Until this moment, with Jack holding me tight to him, I'd never seen a water spirit. They inhabited the old stories, not the waters of our town. They can't possibly be real. At first, I set myself straight: it's only the foxfire playing through the mist and sparking up from the water. There is no other explanation. I don't care that Dalia Doroshenko says they're real. Or that the women on our street — Russians, Ukrainians, Scots, Irish, Germans, Bulgarians — all agree. Any woman you talk to says they're real. They shake their heads and say, *Our poor darlings,* as if they'd lost one of their own; and in a way they have, because we're all tied to each other here in Carminetown. I realize this now: a dark thread pulls us together, some more tightly than others, some left dangling. The tightening, the loosening, this always changes — sometimes barely noticed, sometimes pressing the air from our bodies at night till we can't breathe.

But the panni raklies — I force myself to look. They're splashing each other now, so close to the shore that a jet of water hits my face. The acid and arsenic of Galveston's dead river is corrosive. It burns, it's real. The river spirits, their haunted singing, their eerie cascades of laughter, are these also not real? The stab of horror predicted by Dalia Doroshenko suddenly feels strangely ordinary, as if these girls — slippery, dissolving, abrading cell by cell — could slide into my life. Dalia's voice is in my head: *Don't kid yourself. Them girls aren't from no picture book. Them old stories are living things.*

The river spirits never age; they'll always be frozen in the sharp nanosecond of their final tragedy. Dalia says she knew three who ended up in Nurses Creek. And after this night on the tailings, I won't doubt her about the dead girls. Even with my face buried in Jack's arms, I smell their rot, hear their voices. I lift my head to see the beads of water flying from their hair. *Yes, Dalia, they're real. Too real.*

Two weeks ago Dalia was at the funeral of Elvi Saarinen, the new Food World checkout girl. Everybody liked Elvi. Maire Costello the senior cashier told me about Elvi always saying hello to people in the street, stopping to pet cats, visiting her grandma in the nursing home, posting #caturday pics on weekends. And then, Maire whispered, that boyfriend of hers went and killed her. After it happened, Maire couldn't stop talking about Elvi. She got written up over it, for upsetting the customers.

Oh that poor child, God love her, said Dalia when she'd come straight from the funeral service to the sidewalk in front of our house. Dalia fished the topmost funeral sandwich from her purse and started in about the manhunt for Elvi's boyfriend. It was all over the news. *He did it with a carving knife. Or maybe his hunting knife,* Dalia said, chewing. *Then he rolled her up in a sheet of vapor barrier and put her behind the burn pile.* Dalia let that sink in, swallowed hard, and lowered her voice. *Lucky for him the cops got to him first,* she said, *before our rusalkas.*

Maidens

Rusalkas. That's what Dalia's people call them. Dalia always says, *They came over with us way back when. They swam alongside the boats crossing the ocean, and that's no joke. We need them to keep the men on their toes, and that's no joke either.* Depending on who you talk to, there are many names for these girls. The women say they're as much a part of the town as the living. They settle scores, something the women can't or won't do. Some secretly cheer them on.

"Let's get outta here," whispers Jack, reaching for me, but I can't move. Elvi Saarinen's on the other side of the ferns. She's pulled herself out of the water, perches on a log barely fifteen steps away. "Mama," she's saying, looking around wildly as if she doesn't know where she is. I can't tell the weeds from her hair. "I'm not dead," she says. She doesn't see us. "I'm alive. I have to be."

"Elvi Saarinen?" says Jack. He turns to me, white-faced. "But Elvi's dead."

Elvi, grey-green and dissolving, bends over a cellphone. Where'd she get a cellphone? Can dead girls even use cellphones? The other panni raklies crowd around, the phone screen shining greenish into their faces. Or it's the green of the wreaths braided from river grass and woven into their hair, the girls and grasses decomposing slowly, softening into each other.

When Elvi speaks, her voice is distant, gentle, like water lapping against reeds. She says she'll call Bruno and tell him she loved him, then she'll tell him she wishes she'd never met him, again that she loves him, then that she hates him. She's due to clock in at Food World at 8 a.m., and it's this that seems to push her over the edge. She throws the cellphone into the ferns. Tears pour from her sunken eyes.

"Just wait till Bruno shows up," she says, with a sudden vicious edge to her voice.

Waiting at the shore, tomorrow or the next night or the next, if the stories are true, the panni raklies will sing for Bruno. Except he won't come, even though he'll feel their song like an ache in his bones, an unruly desire. Bruno will be in court. Or in a holding cell somewhere. Dalia says the panni raklies won't be satisfied till he's been released. *Then he better watch out.*

Coral

Now run. Run. But I can't. Nothing in my body will move.

Jack's hand is nearly crushing mine. "What are they?" he whispers.

"River spirits." Is that my voice, dry as leaves?

"River spirits? What the hell are river spirits?"

I can't answer. I'm lost in the water, the girls, the birches on the shore, the stink of rot and death. *Move, move. Back away, turn around, feel your feet on the earth, run, don't walk back into the world, the one you know.* But another girl's speaking now, her voice sparking as if ignited by water. I know this voice.

Ten Stuart Street, red inferno, orange sky, sirens. Screaming from a fiery body, hand pounding at an upstairs window. The house roaring into itself, bursting a red hole in the sky, and in the morning a charred foundation, threads of smoke rising. You're walking down the street one day past the Kowalski house. Next day, nothing but a black hole. Deeper than that hole, all the miners under the ground, digging, tunneling, crying for the dead. Getting drunk at night, crying again, punching the air, sick in the alley behind the Sylvanite Hotel.

I know this girl. It's hard to understand what she's saying, but I think I hear her say *Galveston.*

"My God," says Jack, turning to me. "Is that Gord Kowalski's girl? Is that Coral?"

"Everybody knows why they killed my dad," she's saying, "but at least my sister got out. I miss them every minute of every day."

"It is," says Jack, grabbing for my hand, squeezing it too tight. "It's Coral."

Coral starts again, her voice thin as ashes. "He stood up to them and he wouldn't back down." *Killed my dad everybody knows why.* How many hundreds of times has she spoken her words to the river? *My sister Primrose sister Primrose.* Who has heard? *Every minute of every day.* It has been thirteen months since the fire.

"What the hell?" says Jack. He's rubbing his eyes, hands shaking. Even though I'm shaking too, with Coral's deep horror and grief before me, this softness in him calms me. How many men have seen this with their own eyes, and lived? "Tell me I'm not hallucinating," he says.

Coral turns and swims away, her lament drifting over the water.

Other Things

We reach the edge of the tailings and cross the ditch, the dance gone out of our steps. "What the hell happened back there?" Jack says. How can I begin to tell him about the panni raklies? The role of men is to know nothing. What was I thinking, bringing him here? I'll hear no end of this from Dalia Doroshenko.

We're on the road, finally. A comfort. The plain, solid world. A breeze comes up, the mosquitoes disperse, we're alone under the moon. The trees of the forest are black, their branches embroidered on the sky, and the road unrolls itself into the darkness. No light shines from the windows of the houses.

At my front door, he kisses me, and I feel his lower lip trembling. My mind is still at Nurses Creek, on Coral and the shimmering dead girls. I feel the river, the trees, the ferns, caught in their grief. Life waterlogged. Heavy as a dripping sheet cold in your arms. How to lift it? Maybe you can't, or shouldn't.

The Veil

I'm drinking my morning tea and Dalia Doroshenko marches through the door, parks herself at the kitchen table and says, "I seen you going up there."

Of course she did: Dalia lives behind the curtain at her front window.

She says again, louder, as if I hadn't heard the first time, "I seen you going to Nurses Creek." Even though we're alone, she looks around, checking for imaginary eavesdroppers. "You listen," she says, lowering her voice, "we love them girls but they'll sing a man to his death. Keep your Jack Bachinski away from them. And you. Don't you go near em."

She's trying to scare me.

"You don't mix the living and the dead."

Yes, Dalia, I'm scared but I'm going back there again, Lord knows why. I can swallow my words but my need to return to Nurses Creek rises still.

All I can say is, "We were there and they just came out."

"No," says Dalia, shaking her head. "They don't just *come out.* Them rusalkas don't do anything by accident." She looks at the teapot on the table and then at me. "Milk two sugars," she says. "Now listen here," holding her finger in the air as if testing the weather. "We loved them. We still love them. But they aren't for us. They aren't of our world. They live inside our hearts and memories is all." Her eyes narrow. "They're a danger. Something happens when you die but you're still here." She slurps her tea through the sugar cube clamped in her teeth. "There's danger in being in two places at once, in being alive and dead. Carrying that inside you." She holds out her cup for more tea. "That's what makes you deadly. Opening the veil between the worlds."

"But they're ordinary girls who died, that's all."

"Are you not listening to one word I've said?" says Dalia. Her voice is like a dark cupboard. "They're after you. They want you for something. Lord knows why. Don't fall for it."

The Greenhouse

A new shipment of orchids is waiting on the workbench. I open the boxes, check the rhizomes, the bulbs, the leaves. There are no flowers yet. They'll come. I mark off everything on the list.

> Vanilla planifolia (flat-leaved; lush, overpowering scent of vanilla)

> Cattleya (east-west window or shaded south window; fragrant; not roots but a pseudo-bulb for a water reservoir)

> Pansy orchid (butterfly-designed, a pseudo-bulb at its base)

> Slipper orchid (spotted top petal resembles a disease; sprouts hairs; the lower lip a sullen pouch like it's been sucker punched)

> Moth orchid (wide flattened petals patterned like fractals, rivers, or the blood vessels of a lung)

I shut my eyes to see the future moth orchid in full flower, its markings like a map in satellite view, or from a drone: a river, its feeder streams, the tributaries and deltas. The wild fen orchids don't have such markings. Their patterns are subdued — rivers in miniature. To me, though, they're more beautiful than Galveston's caged orchids.

In the light of day, so much is beautiful. The watery green fen is beautiful. Jack Bachinski is beautiful. Every minute these days, beauty visits me.

Iris

Iris Blythe the housekeeper is sitting in Galveston's kitchen, polishing his silver teaspoons and watching *My New Improved Gypsy Wedding*. I try to ignore it like I ignore all the other shows blaring in the background while she cleans. Like a lot of Carminetown women, she can't get enough of weddings. In the time I've been here, Iris has run through every single reality dating show, wedding show, and now she's started with the B-list stuff.

It's tempting to tell her a thing or two about these "Gypsy weddings," but Mam would say if I did I'd get fired. Not only fired but I'd never get a job anywhere. Not here in town, or the next town over, or the town after that. They'd send us packing. Her go-to warning is always my grade five teacher. *Remember what that teacher did.*

"Wow," says Iris, polishing the same spoon again and again, not taking her eyes from the TV. "Them Gypsies must be loaded." A woman in a white dress wide as a pond is struggling to fit through the door of a gold carriage. I can't even look. Iris asks where did they get the money for them dresses? "Oh right," she says, laughing. "They'd of stole it."

I keep my head down, hold my breath against her, fill my water bottle quickly, and get back to the safety of the greenhouse. The air is cool and humid. Breathe. In, out, in, out. I bring the clay pots and wire nets and orchid medium from the shelves, arrange the roots and rhizomes inside their new nests. I say to the roots: *It isn't Iris's fault. She doesn't know any better. Like everybody in all the towns.*

Later she appears at the door. She's holding a tray with sand-wiches and a pot of tea. I don't know how to sidestep this invitation. I wash my hands in the sink at the end of the green-house, and we sit down to her sandwiches and her tea. Except I don't eat. When she isn't looking, I tear off half my sandwich, put the piece into my pocket. We don't speak. Later she cuts into the silence, telling me about her rented room and her cat who died. She's lost for a few minutes, then yanks herself out of her grief. She laughs and shakes her head and starts in again about the Gypsies.

Iris, you wouldn't know a Gypsy if you saw one. But Iris is just getting started. She goes on to lament the lack of Gypsies in Carminetown. She wants big skirts, bare feet, wild dancing, violins, fire. And she wants shenanigans around the fire, "like in them old romance novels," she says. "You know what I'm talkin about." She moves on to complain about the "reserve girls." She wants them, too, as unbridled as her fantasy Gypsies, to ruffle up the edges of her meager life.

I get up and turn to the workbench so I don't have to look at her. I concentrate on the last tangle of moth orchid roots before me.

"You okay?" says Iris.

My hands tighten around the roots and the end of a rhizome breaks off and falls to the floor.

"What's up?" she says. "Did that stuff about my cat dying upset you? Are you not hungry?"

"No. Thank you." Then, because she sounds hurt, I do what I've learned: I appease, soften, comfort, however angry it makes me. "It's okay, Iris. Everything's fine."

She offers to wrap up the rest of my sandwich so I can take it home.

I make myself say, again, "Thanks, Iris," and she smiles as I take the sandwich. Her pleasant turnip face glows a shade of pink.

At the end of the day, the orchids are unpacked, the roots and bulbs nestled in their new earth. I throw Iris's sandwich into the garbage can.

"Bye," she calls as I leave. She's shaking out a kitchen rug. I don't walk home through the orchid fen. I stick to the streets of Carminetown.

Kissing Jack Bachinski

The nights Jack Bachinski isn't with the guys at the Sylvanite Hotel, I convince him to come to Nurses Creek. Lovely unknown dangers lie ahead, and me without brakes. It's easy to blame Dalia Doroshenko, whose warnings have seeded a dark thrill. As the moon rises, I text him.

> hot for you

His reply flares onto my screen.

> hotter than hot

> hot enough
> for nurses creek?

> you want me hot *and* scared?

> lol on my way

> already here &
> melting for you

I run through the dark to the tailings, and he lifts me up in his arms, a grand romantic gesture I think is more about showing me he isn't scared. He staggers, but doesn't let go.

"Goddamn, you're heavy," he says, veering across the surface.

Even so, we kiss. At first our kisses are small and delicate, but soon they burst open. This is the way of our kisses.

The panni raklies have not returned. Tonight, though, a man appears in the distance, indistinct in the dark. When I pull away, Jack lets me down as gracefully as he can manage.

"That guy, know who that is?" he says. I can't really tell. All I see is that he's sliding on the tailings crust, trying to keep upright, like he's drunk, or reeling with a death wish so close to the panni raklies' river.

"That'll be Galveston's son," Jack says. "Party boy Heron up from the city, slip-sliding all over his dad's dirty tailings." He says you never see Heron when he comes up here, which is hardly ever; he only goes out after dark.

"Heron Galveston?" I've never seen him either, despite how often my mother went on about him. "I wouldn't know him from a hole in the ground."

"You wouldn't want to," says Jack. I don't tell him Heron was her little darling all those years ago.

Watching him career over the surface of the tailings, I think of my mother's codes — of purity, defilement, pollution — and of the horrendous deaths of girls and women. There's no purity anywhere in this place. No sanity or relief. Not for the women or this ruined water or the defiled land. And now nighthawk Heron, the most defiled, sliding across his father's tailings.

Jack shakes his head, pulling me close. "That prick's the one behind the fire," he says.

Ten Stuart Street: the address burned into the dark history of Carminetown. The neighbors had tried desperately to help the volunteer firefighters with their own hoses and buckets, but the flames were raging. The firemen had to soak the roof of the house next door, and fought the blaze all night. In the end, the coroner removed the charred bones of Coral and her father. Primrose, burned, soot-smeared, thin screams coming from her mouth, was taken away in an ambulance.

Where was Heron then?

Now his shadow disappears into the dark, and we hear the slamming of a car door, the revving of an engine.

"That'd be a Porsche," says Jack.

Gallivanting

I hear my mother before I see her. "I am so bloody disappointed in you," she yells into the night. "Out with that gorjo again, weren't you. Gallivanting." She pulls her sweater tight as I climb up our front steps. Her miserable coarse grey two-dollar sweater from the Lutheran Church bazaar, knitted by a miner's wife, worn by three generations of women, and at this moment my mother's shield against me and my transgressions.

I'm still tasting Jack's kiss. "Sorry," is all I can say, and she starts again, finishing up with crying that this gorjo will finish me, and Carminetown is like all the others.

"Carminetown," she spits. "We never should of moved here."

My poor angry mother. I see how diminished she is. She'd wanted the carmine red of sunsets, cardinal flowers, roses, maple trees at the end of September. She imagined red skirts and paisley shawls, her dark braided hair under a flowered diklo. We'd live like the old people, the puri fowki, she told me before we moved here. My mother in her church bazaar shoes, dancing between a hopeless paradise and the harsh sweater of the present. Nobody back home dressed for paradise. You can't hide from the gorjos in a red skirt.

I take her inside. After a long time she stops crying. "I don't want to lose you," she says.

Dark Red

The younger people here want my mother's early version of Carminetown: they've rejected the itchy sweaters and bent shoulders of their grandmothers and great-grandmothers. They plant flowers at the library. Some paint their houses green, blue, yellow, bright red, and long for white picket fences and elm trees in their front yards. It's a nostalgia for friendly streets, for perfect gardens that never existed in this place.

Behind this filigree of hope, Carminetown is a closed chamber with a high dark ceiling and no windows, walls lost in shadow, appearing to recede — but you know the walls are there, keeping you in. The floor of the chamber is unstable with tunnels and shafts and veins of gold running beneath the joists, and the men dig and crawl in these tunnels. Even underground, the mine casts its shadows up into every house, every life.

Despite the desires of the young people, in winter and summer, Carminetown is layered in wool. The formless grey sweaters, long underwear, prickly shawls and skirts and trousers, scarves knotted tightly under women's chins: European immigrant clothing of desperation and hope, the thin threads of not enough and needing more. At night the grandmothers mend the woolen socks shredded at heel and toe. Through the week, the socks wear thin, and again the grandmothers mend. The constant mending of the socks, of everything, goes on day after day, night after night. On laundry days the woolen clothes weigh down the clotheslines, and drip for hours, the drips forming runnels of water in the yards. Over their fences the women whisper about which daughter or cousin or wife has been beaten or betrayed, and about the water spirits — the only ones who can settle the score.

In the struggling women's shelter off Commissioners Road, women with black eyes or swollen jaws pace the fenced back yard where their men can't see them. At night, these men and others gather at the Sylvanite Hotel. In the back room they drink and play blackjack, red dog, poker. Fights erupt from these games that aren't really games. From time to time blood spatters across the pavement at the back of the hotel, but the stains are walked on, rained on, snowed on, and forgotten. My mother, in moving us to Carminetown, had hoped for red, but not that kind of red.

Away

Most of us come from away. Coming with hope across an ocean or from other towns, seeking a new life in this new place with its buried gold, too many of us believing nobody had ever lived here before we came. We invent or erase histories, tell the old fairy tales and myths and come up with new ones. We repurpose lives, gossip, tell stories, but never the truth. Never the darkness. The dark of the mine with its claws in the earth, in the people. The mine batters the men, the men batter the women and children, and the dead take their revenge.

The women from the reserve, if you asked them, they could tell you about the dark. They name the girls and women who go out and never come back. They know the town men who take them.

In the black chamber of Carminetown, a hidden door opens out to a path that takes you to the fen. In the fen there's light. There's life. Whirring air, shifting islets, motes of morning light on transparent wings, a haze of green things unfurling and opening to the sun. I'd rather be at the fen, that place where the laws are true, real, embedded in the underground networks humming from root to root.

Collision

If I could escape my mother's questions, I'd go to Nurses Creek every night to wait for the panni raklies. After seeing them once, I can't get enough. Like me, they're living at the edges, the blurred places between here and there. I know this shifting ground. It's what I'm used to. Dalia Doroshenko says they're after me. That's Dalia and her sweeping paranoia. But she was right about something: there is a thread, an ineffable connection that binds us to each other, the panni raklies and me.

They didn't sing last night. Looking out across the tailings, I saw how they shone under the moon — the reflected drops of water on their skin, dripping green hair, haunted sunken eyes, bodies half-there. Then they submerged and didn't resurface. The water was still.

When I got up to leave, Jack Bachinski was at the far end of the tailings. The night lowered itself around me and I couldn't move. I didn't want to. The world was no bigger than my heart making a mess under my ribs and my trembling knees and the lean of his body toward me. My foot took an involuntary step toward him. Then my body yanked me forward and I was running, slipping on the wet bank, and he was coming toward me too. We collided and landed on the ground and it unfolded from there. I unfolded. Jack, he unfolded too.

What I Remember of Jack's Story, Whispered Two Nights Ago on the Tailings

In search of nectar, a bee enters the orchid. It burrows in through the velvet slipper, and can't find nectar, because there is none. The bee tries to leave, but is trapped in the slipper. *Imagine being hemmed inside the walls of a perfumed prison, with no escape.* The bee must pass under the pollen-coated stigma, and then turn itself around, covered now with pollen, and go out the way it came.

The bee flies from orchid to orchid, its body shrouded in the pollen of every sister of the orchid family. Soon the bee learns there is no nectar to be found. But young bees — ignorant of this dilemma — repeat the cycle, entering the slipper and turning around to leave, weighted down with pollen.

Jack's Gardens

Not one but three gardens grow behind Jack's house. The house, his childhood home inherited from his mother, isn't anything to look at, but I like the small bright rooms that flow into each other. A stream could have been the blueprint, curved lines moving across a blue page. At the back of the house, a quiet bay outside the flow, a separate bedroom looks over the gardens.

Jack invites me to sit at his kitchen table. He makes me tea and sets out a plate of date squares made by his next-door neighbor Irene Slepchik. The date squares are fresh and asking to be eaten. "Have more," says Jack. Because I don't know how to fill the space with talking, I eat. I eat half the plate of date squares.

"Next time," says Jack, "I'll make you wild mushroom soup."

Is he luring me with food? He gathers up the cups. Next time. I want to say, *Did you ask if I agree to a next time?* But my mouth is full and my tongue won't move.

Next time makes me feel drunk. Avoiding Jack's eyes and his *next time*, I look around the kitchen with its pale yellow walls and the sun coming through the window. I've never been inside a man's house before. Mam would kill me if she knew.

Jack takes me out the back door and leads me through the gardens: first, a small meadow of long-headed anemone, bergamot, purple coneflower, summer phlox; then the leaf-filtered light of a birch grove; a hidden slope under the canopy, ending at a stream, and behind the stream the forest. The stream, Jack says, with its cresses and marsh marigolds, is fed by the waters flowing south from the orchid fen. He watches me, eyes unreadable. But his body, I can read that.

I look back at the garden. Does he roll around in it, as he did on the islet in the fen? Is he naked in his garden as he was in the fen? I recall his hand then, running the cotton grasses across his skin, imagine the imprint of his body on the moss. How do you forget the brightness of that? In that brightness, my questions flare up: why me? Why choose me? His eyes still reveal nothing. Maybe it's that he hides behind them as I hide. Jack and Orchid, two soft fen animals, hiding, veiling our fen love — roots tangled under water, careening damselflies, small folded petals of orchids — because the people of the town would not understand. But there's his body, offered up open and shy beside me: the beginning of us. Lying with him, I feel cradled by the fen, even in his backyard garden.

When I get home I call out for my mother. Our house feels disappointing now, the mirror of Jack's built in the rush of Carminetown's expansion, but without the illusion of water, without the gardens. In the kitchen, the dishwasher has been emptied, the dishcloth draped over the kitchen faucet. The floor shining. She must have been up to this while I was gone. The pristine surfaces, scrubbed as if never used or worn, floating over the dark layers of grief and regret. I want to show her Jack's gardens. Shine their light over her sad, angry skin.

All Over Me

"Where were you?"

"Just out."

"You're always just out. What about me?"

"What about you?"

"I need you here."

"No, you don't. You cleaned the whole house by yourself."

"That's because you weren't here. You were with that gorjo. Your face is all puffy."

"Leave me alone."

"Oh, that's what you'd like, isn't it?"

Mam's all over me. Either all over me or off in the clouds. Here/not here.

As we face each other in an expanding silence, I run through the list:

- Leaving me for that job when I was only a kid

- Getting fired, crying in the kitchen while I make breakfast/lunch/supper/sweep floor/ wash dishes

- Walking behind me to school, coming through the classroom door, peering in, all the kids watching her

-   Interrogating me after school: *Who did you have lunch with? Did they pick on you? Did you pass your test? Are you sure you weren't picked on?*

After grade nine, all over me with new interrogations: *Who was that boy you were talking to? Them chavvies can use you, do terrible things — you don't want to know. No you can't go out, not with any of them boys. They're dirty gorjos all of them. You'll wait for a proper Romany mush. Button up your blouse.*

Additionally (sometimes out loud, but always and forever implied): *I won't let them hurt you.*

Who, Mam? Who would hurt me?

Never mind. She says this in a refrain, as if hurting me can be renewed and cautioned against every day. *Them gorjos. They'll hurt you.* She doesn't know about the gorjo boyfriends I had behind her back.

When she's asleep I run to Jack's house. Every night, Jack's house. I come back home in the thin moment between dark and sunrise.

Where r u

are u in the orchid fen

yes

i didn't think youd get reception there

wherever theres orchids theres
reception theyre electrically charged lol

so tell me tell me about the fen today

the air smells of water i see a frog oh a
damselfly boreal bluet it's a male
because of the blue eyes

tell me about it

i have to look it up hang on it says male
blue and black habitat marshy lakes
may to august

where are you

at home come over i have to ask you
something

what do you want to ask me

i dont want to text it

text me anyway

its important

is it an emergency

not really

                            i hate waiting

okay

so

okay so what I want to say is marry me
u r my sky my air my orchid in the fen

Boyfriends

My heart's pounding against my ribs, ready to burst. *Jack Bachinski wants to marry me.* Me, Orchid Lovell, and the beautiful fen-man Jack Bachinski. The floor tilts under my feet. I'm dizzy with him. I can't stand up. Is this what love feels like?

One of the three before Jack wanted to get married. They were all too handsome and never asked questions. They gelled their hair, smoked too much dope, bought lottery tickets, and gave me stuffed animals — the kind you give a child. One of the three had a vinyl siding franchise with a branch in Sudbury. He wanted me to be in awe of his car, a 1961 Lincoln Continental coupe convertible with red leather seats. That's the only thing I remember about him.

None of these men could see me. I tried to see them but it was difficult with their expectations and loud voices and drugstore smells. They thought it was funny that I loved the fen. I never lasted more than six months with any of them. Why did I even go out with them? To feel wanted? To get away from my mother?

Yes

Jack comes to my door and gives me a letter. "Don't read it right away. Wait till bedtime." He turns red, averts his eyes. We stand in our secret silence, my mother quietly snoring in her bedroom.

I read the letter as soon as he leaves. Some words have been crossed out and replaced, some underlined. *What I love in you: You're older than the fen. Through your eyes the world is a wonder. Your hands in the crumbling black soil are beautiful to see. Your feet standing in the water of the fen like roots into the earth. Like my roots. You see the dead river girls and don't turn away. You see things as they are.*

I lie across my bed, holding the letter over me as I read and reread his words, and imagine answers. *I'm weak for you. Also strong. I see you the way you see me. I love you like the fen, like the electrical pulse in its mycelium veins. Like the orchid's lip opening. I think that's how I love you. I don't know enough about love to feel or say the right things. I'm not good at having feelings that crowd me or that I don't understand. I follow our ways. Most of them. What ways, you might ask. There are three things: pure, dirty, and defiled. You will have to learn this.* I text him as soon as I can gather these thoughts into a single word.

My answer is Yes.

Mosquito Wedding

We can't decide where to get married: orchid fen or the tailings at Nurses Creek. Our guests will be mosquitoes and blackflies and our mouths, orchid-lipped, pollen-drenched, will swell from being bitten and kissed.

We decide on the fen. Human guests — Dalia Doroshenko, my mother, Jack's next door neighbor Irene Slepchik, Lennie Pomerantz who fixes his truck, and everybody from his shift — all boycott the wedding. Nobody in their right mind, they say, would get married in a swamp. Especially with the mosquitoes and black-flies, which in case we hadn't noticed are the worst they'd ever been on account of how hot it is these days. We bribe Willard Honecker the JP, who is angry at having to come out here. His temper is sweetened by the offer of extra cash. We have to pay the two scowling witnesses as well: his twin sisters clearly itching to spread the news of this outrage.

Standing knee-deep in the bog, Willard rushes through the ceremony, dropping the rings in the water. Still, it's beautiful. I've made a wreath of marsh grasses for my hair, and bought a white dress from the 50% off rack at the back of Edna's Brides. Jack, chiselled, dark, smelling of water and orchids, wears his black fedora and his dad's old tux, two sizes too small. Willard Honecker's muttering under his breath, "Will you just find the goddamn rings."

In the middle of all the commotion I'm distracted by a shadow that flits behind an islet and under the branches of a birch tree. A splash, light high laughter. An arm above the water, a sharp hollow face, then another, green hair pooling. The panni raklies are here: sly witnesses to the wedding. Are they tracking me, filming my wedding on their cellphones? Whatever their intent, in a way I'm glad they're here. A friendly presence, a kind of validation of our love.

As if on cue, the rings are found, and pushed onto our shaking fingers.

When it gets to the part about *with my body I thee worship* we're practically champing at the bit, restrained by unseen hands. Willard Honecker must notice. He reads through that part at a clip, as if outraged at our bridled bodies. In our delirium — brought on by our desire and by blackfly venom in our blood — we rise, floating over the fen, our feet grazing the tops of the trees.

Willard Honecker is down there swatting at the insects and saying, "Can we get the hell out of here?"

List

We go to my place. My mother is at her bedroom window. She's watching the moon, and turns around only long enough to glare at Jack.

"Shut the door," she says. Jack's stuck out in the hall, helpless, patient, scared, scratching at the bites at his ankles and wrists. Probably listening from the other side of the door. Mam keeps her voice down — she won't give him the satisfaction — and starts going through the list:

> — First of all, what if my cancer comes back? Where will I go? What will happen to me if you're not here?

Then:

> - Looks like a goddamn movie star. That's a red flag right there.

> - Plenty of women I'll bet. What does he do with them all?

> - You should be marrying one of our own. He knows nothing about our fowki. About our ways. Mixing the mokkadi, the defiled, with the pure and the clean, it'll only end in grief. My tikni shey ruined.

"Did you tell him? You know what I'm talking about. Did you tell him who we are?" *Tell him so he'll reject you.* This is veiled by her words, all her words, all the time: *Don't tell them who we are,* but today it's, *Did you tell him who we are?* I hadn't said a thing. Our secret still has its hands tight around my throat.

I lie. "Yes, I told him."

In our wedding aftermath, I speak to her every day. I come to the house with Jack. I make her sit at the table across from him. He brings offerings: flowers from the garden, his next door neighbor's date squares.

"I know what's going on," she says. "Trying to butter me up, he is." I tell her, finally, that because I am now married, I will move into Jack's house with him.

"You two can go wherever the hell you like. Go live with that man."

"His name is Jack."

"Whatever."

Shopping

- bed (queen size)
- sheets 2 pr
- pillowcases 4 pr
- pillows 4
- duvet
- curtains
- bathroom towels 6
- dish towels 6
- dishcloths 8
- paint, brushes
- rollers
- drop cloth

We argue about the paint for the bedroom. I want indigo for night, he wants red for hot love. We end up with boring off-white.

A compromise: one pair red sheets, one pair deep blue. Everything loaded into the back of Jack's truck. He wants to fly the red pillowcase out the window, like a flag, as we drive home through the town. He wants to stop at the Sylvanite, show off our bed. We argue about this on the way to Food World. I tell him our bed is private; he says he wants to show it off to the guys, to the town. Why would you need to do that? I ask. He says he wants every-body to see our love. I tell him our love is not a flag to be waved in the streets. "Okay okay okay," he says, throwing up his hands. He waits in the truck, guarding our bed while I go into Food World with my list: tea, coffee, sour cream, sugar, flour, lard.

Maire Costello is at the checkout. "Look," she says, ignoring my pile of shopping. "Over there." She shakes her head. "Can you believe it?" I'm sensing strong disapproval, a welcome diversion from Jack and the bed. "There goes that Queenie. The little bitch."

A girl, silver, beautiful, thin like a sapling, flits down the aisle. She's like a vision from the fen.

"Have you not seen Queenie?" says Maire. She whispers that Queenie is a nurse who turns her patients into frogs or trees or some such. Or her patients are already frogs or trees or whatever and they don't yet know it.

"That's garbage, Maire."

"I kid you not."

I don't repeat any of this to Jack.

The women of the street gather to watch as we back into the driveway, and Irene Slepchik brings out her upstart nephew Cyril Lepke to help get the bed off the truck. A couple of the women nudge each other and laugh. When they announce in loud voices that this bed will see plenty of action, I want to hide.

Cyril hands me his mother's date squares in a tin. "For the lovebirds," he says, looking slyly at Irene.

"The nerve," she says later, glaring at her sister's rival date squares.

Not Moving

In Jack's house — now our house — we cook supper, sweep the floor, load the dishwasher, then go at it till dawn, on the bed, floor, sofa, wherever we fall. The legs of the new box spring collapse. We shore it up with two-by-fours and the ends of logs from Jack's back garden. The wood cracks and the logs slip. The bed breaks again. Every three days we fix the bed.

At night, Irene Slepchik bangs on our window, hollering for us to keep it down. The third night Jack wants to yell back at her, but I tell him, Irene is your good neighbor, she brings you date squares. Only when Lennie Pomerantz comes to relay complaints from the street do we finally know we'll have to be quiet because Lennie owns the garage where Jack gets his truck fixed, and therefore Lennie is God.

On the weekend when Jack goes to make peace with Irene, I return to my mother's house, sit at her kitchen table.

"You're coming with me. You only need to stay five minutes, but you are coming."

She refuses to put on her shoes. She goes out the door in her bare feet.

At our house, Jack holds out his arm to help her up the steps. She won't look at him. I show her the back bedroom with its screen door that opens out to the garden. "What's all that out there? I want to see. Only look, mind. I'm not moving in."

Wild ginger is everywhere. Violets. Bergamot, coneflower, salvia shivering with bees. We step down into the birch grove with its fractured green air. "It's like I'm under water," she says. We go to the stream, where she picks and eats the watercress growing in the shallows. Back at the house, she stands again in the open door, looking over the garden. She turns to me. "I can only dream of having a garden like this." Then she gets snappish again. "I'm not moving in."

✦

The next morning, as I'm leaving for work, she calls. "Murri shey," she says, her words faint, as if spoken from another room. When I arrive I find her in bed, curled in on herself like a caterpillar.

She holds her hands to her stomach and says, "It's nothing."

I offer her soup. She shakes her head, pushing herself up. She won't let me help her, but walks stiffly, bent, clutching at the walls.

"It's just a stomach ache," she says, stumbling back into her room. "Indigestion. All that food of his you made me eat." She shuts the door.

Is she faking it? It wouldn't be the first time.

Jack sends me a text. **Where are you?**

I call off work and stay with my mother till she goes to bed. I dread to think the cancer has come back.

Supper

On Saturday I bring her to sit in Jack's garden.

At supper she tells me, "I won't eat with that mush."

"His name is Jack."

"Whatever."

"He's a good cook, Mam."

"Never mind."

Jack brings her tea. He brings her crepes stuffed with wild mushrooms and sorrel. He pours cheese sauce over the crepes. "I will have one bite only," she says. She eats the one bite and pushes away her plate.

Later we go out to the garden again. She lowers her face to the milkweed flowers. She bends down to the wintergreen and pipsissewa, and calls back to me. "Look," she says, "this one's for headache," and sinks her teeth into a wintergreen leaf. Inside, Jack shows her his collection of jars filled with wild medicines, each one labeled. She reads the names aloud. When she sees Jack watching her she says to the ceiling, "Typical. Gorjo thinks he knows everything," and asks to go home.

A Rose

It started with hiding my greenhouse job from Mam, finding winding routes to work so Dalia Doroshenko wouldn't know, moving quickly through the streets to where the rich people live.

I dislike their mansions, menacing and judgemental, with no satisfying human commotion inside the gardens or walls. The streets are shaded and lush, but not in the way of the fen. They emanate an ominous hush, and are nearly always empty except for the people from the town who come to mow the lawns and trim the hedges. The owners of the mansions don't sit out on their porches or stand around talking in the road, but keep their social lives away from the rest of us. I got the lowdown on these people and their habits from Irene Slepchik.

This morning, I dare to enter their park. It's overgrown with tamed roses that climb around benches and over trellises. I'm not alone. On the rose-bordered path, a man leans against a tree. He's talking on a cellphone and looks over at me, tilting his head to watch my progress, dark hair falling over his forehead. My stomach doesn't like this scrutiny, but short of turning around, there's nowhere for me to go. I've seen that look before, or something like it, in Jack's imitation of the mine bosses. But there's something more here too, something heady, rose-scented, dripping. I've seen that look before too.

The man pinches off a reddish coral rosebud and holds it out to me as I pass. I don't know what else to do, so I take it.

"I've not seen you here before," he says with a half-smile. "It'll be our secret."

He's polished and beautiful, this man is. Dark, graceful. His voice is low. He must belong to this park; he has that look about him. When he turns back to his cellphone, I rush past him along the path, crushing the rosebud inside my fist. I don't want to go to work. I want to go to Nurses Creek, to the panni raklies, tell them the secret I have been ordered to keep.

Sweeping

In the greenhouse, I fall asleep at the orchid table. Iris comes in with her sandwiches and pot of tea. She stops and looks at my hand. "Omygod, is that a wedding ring?"

"Yes."

When I tell her my husband's name, she says "Jack! All the girls love Jack Bachinski." The bright disappointment in her eyes tells me she might love him too.

She sets her tray on the table. "I almost got married," she says, sitting down to make room for her story. At fifteen she had a boyfriend for a night. Before he did it to her, he told her he loved her and that they'd get married. She describes the dress she wanted, the one she saw in the front window at Edna's Brides, the skirt filling the whole display. Fourteen weeks later her mother ended up having to take her to the doctor.

She picks up a broom and pushes the dirt away from the table, sweeping so fast that dust flies everywhere. As she sweeps, she describes the day's TV episode and what they're wearing. "That goddamn dress had to be ten feet wide," she says with a laugh.

"I'm not interested in weddings," I say.

"But you just got married!" she laughs, and stops when she sees my dark look. "Sorry," she says, shrinking. She goes back to her sweeping. Like my mother, she sweeps and sweeps over the same place, back and forth, painfully.

The stranger's rose in my pocket is bruised and limp, and I throw it into the yard.

Telling

The cotton grass grows matted, Labrador tea leaning over the shore. The humming fen is washed with gold. At the end of July the mosquitoes retreat, and on a cool night we sneak out to sleep under the trees by the fen. Deep in the forest, night sounds become lace.

"I have to tell you something about myself."

Jack turns to me in the half-dark. "Okay," he says, a question mark in his voice.

"I'm the same person I was five minutes ago. I'm the same person now."

He says now I'm scaring him. First I tell him about the moving. This town and all the others. I think we moved every two years or so. I remember Tillsonburg, then Hamilton, then Orillia. Further and further north, we landed and did not fit, according to my mother, who gave no reason. Gravenhurst, Parry Sound, Sudbury. We never got found out, although my mother always insisted we had to leave before it happened.

"What do you mean 'found out?'"

"In Magenta Falls, the town before this, we were found out."

"What were you? Drug dealers? Bank robbers?" He's laughing nervously.

"Worse," I say.

I tell him the casual jokes. *I better watch my wallet around you.* Then the darker stuff: *dirty nymphomaniac, thief, scamming Gypsy crook.*

Botany

It's nearly twelve years ago. I'm ten years old, in grade five. I have a teacher I love. Her name is Miss Dvorak. Miss Dvorak has flax-blue eyes and blond hair, and speaks with an unusual, lilting accent that makes me love her even more. The girls copy her hairstyle. We laugh her high, light laugh. We imitate her way of walking and her gestures, to be more like her.

In our grade five class we're studying plants. What is the same? What is different? What does difference mean? Is one better, one worse? Do better or worse even matter in nature? Miss Dvorak asks us to look at things the way a fly might. Closely, and through many thousands of lenses.

We draw cross sections of flowers. Today a crocus, with labeled parts. Stigma. Anther. Style. Receptacle. Sepal. Stamen. Petal.

"Very good," says Miss Dvorak, looking at my drawing. "Very good, Orchid. Your mother named you well." She holds up my drawing for the class to see. At her desk she predicts my future: scientist, botanist, artist, mathematician. "Anything," she says, the warmth of her smile radiating. "You can be anything."

At home I look up botanist. Aloud I say, "Orchid Lovell, botanist." I make a list of the work a botanist can do.

Study plant evolution

Study plant reproduction

Understand plant relationship to environment

Observe plant growth

Record plant distribution

Grow plants in greenhouse

Protect and monitor plants

etc.

At school I show the list to Miss Dvorak. She nods. *Very good, Orchid.* She says *initiative, gifted, ambition.* She lowers her voice so that only I can hear, suggesting that other students may not have these qualities. I go home and look up *initiative* and *ambition,* to be sure what they mean. I look in the mirror and say them to my reflection.

Orchid Lovell, gifted botanist.

The next week, after plants, we study geography. Miss Dvorak puts a map on the wall, and we are asked to put pins in the countries where we were born, where our parents or grandparents were born. Cities, forests, towns, mountains, suburbs, roads. Each pin representing the people living in those places. How they're shaped by the land. By their work. By the food they eat, their DNA. Cell, membrane, aorta, blood, ventricle. Ulna, tibia, sternum, rib. We're all the same, we're all different, we're all the same. This is what Miss Dvorak tells us.

Soon the map is dotted with pins. England, where I put my pin, is crowded, but more crowded are those countries across the seas and channels: Portugal, Italy, Macedonia, Bosnia, Slovakia, Czech Republic, Poland, Ukraine, Russia. *How wonderful that we come from many places,* says Miss Dvorak, *and that we bring our languages and cultures, our ideas and mementos with us.*

Dishes. That's what my mother brought. Plates and cups and saucers with their dizzying patterns like the oxbow rivers and winding paths followed by our fowki back home.

Miss Dvorak is from Europe. Most of the kids are too. She asks us to tell the class about ourselves. Our homework: write about the people we come from, our beliefs, the beliefs of our parents, grandparents, those things that matter to us. Those things Mam says I'm not allowed to tell. But I'm safe with Miss Dvorak. *We're all the same, all different. All things have value. All life.*

I stand in front of the class and read toward Miss Dvorak's smile. Her words, her kindness have made me who I am in that moment. I'm brimming with gratitude. My secret evaporates. I read aloud the story of my mother, her Romany fowki. Traveling along the roads, stopping to cook their suppers over the yog, sleep under the kushti kali ratti, the beautiful black night.

I remember looking up from my paper to Miss Dvorak. Her smile is gone. When I continue reading, my words pile up like stones. A dark curtain has lowered itself over my teacher's eyes. Even the whites have turned black.

The room, too, is black. The black of my beautiful dark night has become a void. Overturned. Where is Orchid the botanist? I no longer exist.

Kamav Tu

"I'm married to a Gypsy," says Jack with delight. For a minute I fear a repeat of Iris's lurid fantasies. That word. *Gypsy*. Remembering my silence with Iris, I find I'm able to explain that it's a word only for my people to say, that the others should call us Romanies. "Am I one of the others?" asks Jack. How do I answer this? He doesn't ask again. We lie side by side under the trees. We fall asleep. Later, a thin rain wakes us.

We take the shortcut back to his truck. Our feet lift and sink, lift and sink in the earth of the bog as we run through worsening rain.

"You can say it out loud," he says, "tell it to the fen."

Somewhere on my way to Jack's truck, a cloud rises from my body and is dispersed. Under the dark sky I'm filled with light. I weigh nothing. We both shout at the night. *Orchid Lovell is a Romany girl* echoes back from the far shore of Orchid Lake. The sky is heavy. The rain is heavy.

◆

I failed Miss Dvorak's class. I never got to tell my mother's stories of migrations, terrors, being chased from one town, then another and another. Or her stories of hop-picking and flower selling, eating and singing around the fire. Or the story of stories: her dream of a paradise in this country. A mythical place without shadows.

Mam was cornered at work. Word got out and people piled on, even those she'd thought of as friends. *We're only joking,* they said. Mam wasn't exactly fired, but she may as well have been. She was asked to leave because people felt threatened by her presence, and firing would look racist. That's what her one friend told her.

Without a job, she couldn't pay the rent, and again we got told to leave. I remember believing it was my fault. The landlord's face, when he came to the door, said *Sorry not sorry.* In bed, I cried. Mam brought out our boxes and suitcases. We packed our clothes and our dishes with the blue and gold and orange rivers. We left that town and came to this one. She chose it for the color. Carmine. The most beautiful red. *You see,* said my mother. *We don't tell who we are, and that's why.*

But Jack's voice is in my ear. *Say it loud.*

I turn to him and tell him, "Kamav tu." *I love you.* I'm sure I mean it. I've never said it before, not to my mother, not to anybody. Crammed in the front seat of the truck we make orchid love, water love, moth love, damselfly love. We're a messy tangle, a mob of fen creatures rolling through leaves and stems and layers of love.

✦

In the morning before work, I go to see my mother. She's sitting in the kitchen drinking coffee. I bring my chair to her side of the table. In my arms, she's like glass. Her shoulder bones jut. Her wrists are twigs. I say it to her too. *Kamav tu kamav tu.* These words make her cry a bit.

"I think I'll go outside today," she says, looking out the window.

Kamav tu. Kamav tu.

Pie 1

Irene Slepchik invites me over for tea, warning that this is no ordinary occasion: she's bringing out the good dishes. "I want you to meet my young friend," she says. When I arrive, she's sitting in her kitchen with Rose Commanda. Between them on the table sits a plate of date squares, and Irene issues another warning: the date squares are not hers. They are inferior ones made by her sister Ida Lepke, delivered this morning by Ida's son Cyril. Rose doesn't seem to mind the date squares. She's eating happily as I sit down across from her.

Rose is round-faced like her lawyer auntie Marjorie Commanda, the Elder interviewed last week by a regional reporter. The interview was about the importance of preserving wetlands, and Marjorie was all over the TV here and even on the national news. Irene says the white people are scared of her, especially the mine owners and the other baro shatos. In the interview, Marjorie, a small woman, filled the screen as she calmly answered the reporter's questions. She looked bigger than she does in real life, but that's the way it is on TV.

Rose and Irene take three blueberry pies from the oven. Rose says they picked the berries back of the fen. As the pies cool, we sit around the table drinking tea. Chatting about the season's berry harvest, gossiping about unrest among the miners, we nearly finish off one of the pies, even though it's still hot.

Irene takes a swig from her cup and looks at me with the narrowed kind of glare I sometimes got from Dalia Doroshenko. "You were over at the tailings. Visiting them dead girls."

"They're just ordinary girls."

"Ordinary, yes," says Irene. "But what ordinary girl wouldn't be dangerous, holding all them memories of her last breath?" She puts down her cup. "You don't know the half of it. You're still young, and you're not from here. We women in this town, we want them girls to be dangerous. They carry our feelings. They do what we'd do if we had half the nerve."

"You'd be killers?"

"An eye for an eye," Irene says darkly. She starts wrapping up a pie for me to take home.

"I know about those kinds of men," says Rose, whose voice gets suddenly hard. They call across the street, she tells us, offering rides or stealing girls from the reserve, taking them to the Great Lakes boats docked in the ports.

We stop eating. We look at each other and don't speak. What can we possibly say?

✦

When Jack is asleep, I leave our warm bed and run to Nurses Creek with the last piece of pie. Holding the crumbs of Rose's words, the pie is full of more than berries and sugar. I put it down on the shore and wait for the panni raklies.

"I'm here," I call out over the empty river.

Kerosene

When I take the sheet off the clothesline, and my t-shirt rides up over my stomach, Rose comes around the side of the house calling hello, pretending not to see the scars. They're pale now, hardly there. I never told Jack. He hasn't noticed.

The need to explain is inescapable, even though she doesn't mention it. "I was eleven. It was a long time ago," I say.

All Rose says is, "Yeah, I saw that in you."

I feel oddly relieved. She hasn't judged me. We don't say anything more, and slide past the moment, but the memory of that sharpened paring knife in my eleven-year-old hand has taken over, and I have to walk. Anything to keep from standing there. Soon we're on the road into town, passing by Dalia Doroshenko's yard. "That place there?" says Rose. "She used to run a boarding house for miners. My mother worked there when she came off the reserve. Her first day the old lady made her bend over the sink, and washed her hair with kerosene."

Dalia is in the window, her fingers kneading the edge of the curtain. Dalia, who fed me hot dogs and put me to bed when my own mother was gone. Who came to me when I had a bad dream, and said *It's okay, child.*

"That's her," says Rose.

"Why would she do that?"

"She said it was to kill lice," says Rose. "My mother didn't have lice. None of us did."

I close my eyes and see myself banging on Dalia's door and screaming in her face.

Rose is reading my mind. "Don't," she says.

Somewhere

I go to my mother's for the third time this week. It still feels strange that this was once my home. It feels small, temporary, pared down in the way our other houses were when we had to pick up and leave. When I step into the front hall, there is only the creaking of bare linoleum under my feet.

"Orchid? Is that you?"

There is no tea or food on the kitchen table in front of her. Only a folded piece of paper, wrinkled and torn at one edge, alongside a pile of more papers. I sit, and for a long time she doesn't speak. Not even to complain.

"I was just cleaning," she says. "Can you believe I found this, from all them years ago." Unfolding the paper, she slides it across the table. On the page, drawn in hesitant lines, a boy holds the hand of a woman. Hearts fly from the mouth of the boy, whose face is turned up to gaze at the woman. In awkward letters angled across the top of the page: *I love you JadeMarie from Heron.*

"Before you ask," she says, "yes, I have your old drawings too, around here somewhere."

Prophecy

When Jack is asleep, I go to Nurses Creek to ask the panni raklies about Heron Galveston. Coral Kowalski, at the edge of the river, still sings her lament. I know they all know Heron, or his father, or his father's father. *Galveston Galveston* ripples through these waters. The others have come across the river to join her, whispering urgently. I hear *gold*. I hear *Orchid Lake*.

"Let me check," says Elvi, who climbs onto her log at the shore. With the light of the cellphone cast across her body, she scrolls, reading snippets aloud. After a minute the phone flashes a warning. She looks up. "Sisters," she says. "It's a red alert. Gold has been found at Orchid Lake. The Galvestons are starting explorations."

This is the first I've heard of it. Rose never mentioned the government's duty to consult about a new mine. There has been no talk of it about town. This can only be a kind of prophecy, the panni raklies doing their dukkering, foretelling the future. They might very well have been sent these warnings from the fen.

"I can see them two Galvestons right now," says Coral, "face down in the river."

Looking into the water, I can almost see it too: father and son, rocking side by side in the quiet green miasma of Nurses Creek. The vision stirs something inside me.

On the shore, the pie I'd left has collapsed, untouched. The panni raklies' pie-eating days are over. Revenge is their food. The cells of their greying bodies are organized around it. Without revenge they'd be nothing more than rows of bones in the ground.

When I stand, trembling and dazed, Elvi's face turns toward me. The panni raklies are perfectly still in the water around her. My shaking hand sets a new offering on the river bank by the ferns: the body of a dried damselfly wrapped in cotton. A beautiful thing found in the fen, a blue-green needle, metallic brightness reflected under the moon.

At home I sit at the kitchen table. It's three in the morning and I can't shake the crawling feeling that Dalia Doroshenko was right. They were waiting for me, for my offering. I don't know if what I gave them was the damselfly or myself.

The Effects of Gold Mining on Damselflies and Wetlands

Calopteryx maculate, ebony jewelwing, 39 – 57 mm. Metallic body of emerald green, black wings.

> The damselfly alights on a reed at the edge of a shaded stream. The reed bends, not under the weight of the insect, but with the movement of the air. The slightest of breezes causes the reed to tremble or sway, and the damselfly with it. The male perches in the sun dapples, in order that his green body and black wings will be more visible to the female (Lake 2001, 79).

Calopteryx aequabilis, river jewelwing, 43 – 59 mm.

> Again, a body of metallic green, wings of laced veins tipped with black, as if ink-dipped. The jewelwing lives near streams, rivers, the forest edge.

Lestes forcipatus, sweetflag spreadwing, 33 – 44 mm.

> He grasps his lover behind her head and awaits her assent. If accepted, he lifts his secondary genitalia

to meet her vulvar plate, and they make a heart-
shaped flying wheel, their desire rippling in full
flight across the marshy islets (Smaller 1997, 293).

The female, her ovipositor tipped to the moist
earth or into the waters of the fen, deposits the
eggs in the marshes where she lives (Lake 2001).

The wetland is threatened. Then destroyed. A mine
is built. Industry will use bodies of water to dispose
of its waste — tailings, overburden, rock — all that
obstructs the success of the mine. The diggers and
gougers move in, ripping through the muck and
soil, annihilating the damselfly nursery. The eggs
die long before the building of the tailings pond
(Overleigh 2021, 127).

References

Lake, Ro-Anne. 2001. *The Reproduction of Despair and
     Hope*. Fairchild, Wessex and Fontaine.
Smaller, Lavinia. 1997. *Origins of Desire in Northern Orchid
     Fens*. Jansons, Fugler and Smith.
Overleigh, P.K. 2021. "The Effects of Gold Mine Tailings
     and Chemicals on Damselfly Reproduction in
     Northern Ontario." *The Interdisciplinary Journal of
     Biodiversity, Species at Risk, and Endangered Habitats*
     5(9): 115-132.

Overburden

Jack comes home from work dirty and tired. He smells of the mine: airless, with heavy notes of earth and metallic sweat. Ore, he says, was found at the far end of Orchid Lake. He heard it at lunch. Cradled in the ore is a thin vein of gold. Where there's one vein, Jack tells me, there'll be more.

He goes for a shower and comes out after what seems like hours. "Hot," he says, turning on the burner under the soup, and I don't know if he's talking about the heat of the mine, the heat of the shower, or the heat of the stove. He stands there, exhausted, stirring.

"You know what this means," he says later as he sets the table, ladles soup into my bowl. I study the soup, bigger than the bowl it's in. Bigger than the table, the kitchen, bigger than Orchid Lake. A small thing bigger than the sum of its parts: wild blue chanterelles from the forest, the spoonful of sour cream from Food World, from a dairy in the next county, onions from the back garden. Such details are important at a time like this. When I heard this news from the panni raklies, I could convince myself it was only a story. But now, to hear it from Jack — Jack makes it real.

Gold at Orchid Lake. I look down at the floor to make sure it's still under my feet. That it won't swallow me as Galveston's new mine will swallow the fen.

We don't clear the dishes. In bed we lie side by side, numb with this news, pretending to sleep. In the morning, because it's Saturday, we go to the orchid fen. We follow the shore to the far end. Jack waves his arms at the trees. Then he waves his arms wider, at the trees behind those trees.

"All this," he says, shaking his head, inconsolable. "It's all going."

The nuisance layer. Overburden. That's what they call it. The backhoes and bulldozers will open their jaws to scrape away this living layer, and then the drilling begins. Everything goes. Trees, sprouts, topsoil, leaf mold, lichen, mosses, frogs, birds' nests, lilies, bulrushes, turtles, orchids. The perching islets, the sedges, cedars, marsh grasses, water snakes, fishing spiders, wolf spiders, fairy shrimp, the one-celled beings pulsing through the water. Then the mine shaft, gaping mouth, dark swallowing throat to the stomach of the earth, and Mister Galveston's bottle of champagne sprays everywhere.

Two Dreams

Dream 1

Black earth of the shore. Gold under the orchids, spread out in a sheet that stretches from there to here and back again. Wherever *there* is. Sparrow's egg lady's slipper. Pink lady's slippers spread over the spruce swamp. On the north shore, the spotted orchids. Nearby, the small round-leaved orchids.

The panni raklies turn to me. They open their mouths. *Careful*, they say all together. *Don't step on them.*

In the dream I'm with Jack, picking spotted orchids and lady's slippers and braiding them into his long, long hair. Jack and Orchid, lying on the shore of Orchid Lake, our feet in the shallow waves, the swallows darting overhead. I am inside and outside of every part of this dream. Inside the gold, the shining sheet beneath the orchids, holding up their roots.

They're on the road to Orchid Lake. The panni raklies are singing another lament. A dream lament, or their real voices coming through our bedroom window. Maybe it's their prophetic telepathic app, sending their message through the cloud.

They're digging up the yellow bullshead lilies, the pitcher plants, the sprays of pink orchids. They're tearing down the trees full of hummingbirds, flattening the cranberry islets. The winter ice will melt. The marsh will be mullered for a tailings pond. It's what they do.

These places, these beings are already uprooted, shifted sideways into some dream universe. I can smell Orchid Lake before the Galvestons expel their black smoke and spew their tailings, back when cedars and tamaracks lined the marsh. I see the herons, slow and heavy in flight, the shining otters, water snakes and turtles basking on warm rocks. I lie flat on the bank, put my face in the water that tastes of fish and water plants. It's too real.

Girls and women and the land, it's all the same to the Galvestons, the panni raklies sing.

Dream 2

They're surrounding a coffin. Orchid Lake floats inside the coffin suspended above the lower world. The panni raklies stand over the grave, an abyss carved out of the hollow earth. Like the miners' cage, the coffin descends. The hole will widen and swallow everything balanced on its lip: the people of the town, the houses, yards, laundry on the clotheslines, mailboxes, children's tricycles, TV aerials, sidewalks, river tributaries, forests, the fen, our garden, our bed. I call out to the panni raklies but my words, too, disappear into the hole.

"Hey," says Jack. "Wake up. You're screaming."

Crying

When I arrive at my mother's house, I call but she doesn't answer. In her room, she's sitting on the edge of her bed, rocking back and forth. She doesn't see me. Her hands are wet, clamped against her mouth as if holding something in. It takes time for me to understand that she is crying. When she finally sees me, she smooths her skirt, her hair, runs her hands across her face.

"I'm losing my girl." The words are muffled, her voice a child's voice. "I don't want to lose my girl." She reaches out and I step into the circle of her arms. She pulls me close. She's crying against my stomach. Her tears against my scars. I sit down on the bed. We rock beside each other. Who is the mother? Who is the child?

Beyond her room, beyond our house, the panni raklies wait for killers in their viscous river. The miners of the night shift dig and dig. The Galvestons plan their assault on Orchid Lake. Their new mine sends its ghost tentacles under the fen.

A text comes in on my phone.

   where are you?

       at home with my mother

  again?

This *again* makes me angry. Angry on behalf of my mother. I have never before felt anything on her behalf.

When I get home it's dark and Jack is waiting for me. His fingers are laced tightly on the table in front of him and he starts right in. Why am I even living with him when I'm never here? I yell that he's always out with his friends. He says he loves me. He says maybe I don't love him. Maybe he is half right. I'm new to this kind of love. I don't trust it. I don't know what to expect. Mother love I know. I don't like my mother but I love her.

Berries

Mam has not left her bed. I want to cry, seeing her twisted under the sheet, her hair stuck to her face. Did she stumble into my dream of two nights ago, feeling the ghost mine, the death of Orchid Lake? Or maybe Dalia Doroshenko has already told her. I kneel at her bedside and stupidly promise that she'll be okay, that we'll save the fen. She doesn't answer.

By the time I'm out of the house, the Orchid Lake story has already travelled through the streets. I hear it from Irene Slepchik, from other neighbors along the way. The town is divided: half say yes to the mine and half say no. The people from this latter half — most of them women — point out that it isn't Galveston's land to begin with. It's unceded territory. Irene says Rose's aunt Marjorie and the Elders are already gathering their legal team.

Rose and I walk as far as the ditch by the tailings. "Look," she says. "This was never theirs. The land belongs to itself. But we can't walk on it freely any more." She sends her arm wide, gesturing to the trees at the other side of the tailings, to the forest rolling beyond these trees. "My great-grandma used to pick berries every-where here," she says. "Raspberries and blackberries. And further up, that's where they caught brook trout. There, and other places. Look at the river now." Nurses Creek is greenish grey in the after-noon light. Yellow foam skitters across the stolen water.

Rose clears her throat. "Orchid, for a long time I've wanted to tell you something," she says. "It's my cousin who's in there. Coral." Rose's voice catches. "My Coral."

I say nothing. Words are too much and not enough.

"I can't stay here." After the briefest of glances toward the creek, Rose keeps walking. "We were kicked off this land for his mine. My Coral and her dad were killed for his mine. Now it's happening again," she says. "It's always happening."

Silence

Jack and I eat our supper in silence. The only sounds are the clatter of knives and forks against our plates, the scrape of my chair, the pouring of water into our glasses. The air's heavy. I want to tell him that too much of this world is coming at me right now, but there's no room for words. No room for the mine, for our fight, for my mother.

Later, when I call her, she picks up the phone but doesn't talk, only breathes. I tell Jack I'm going to stay with her. He says, "I'll miss you."

I say, "This is not about you."

When I'm through the door at her house, I find her in the bathroom, vomiting with pain. I call Jack and we take her to Emergency. They put her on a gurney and wheel her upstairs for a CT scan. I stay in the hospital all night, sleeping in a chair beside her bed. In the morning before work, I meet with the doctors. They tell me she has a tumor. Sometime soon they will open her up, lift out her uterus, and staple her back together again.

I imagine her orphan uterus and its parasite in the doctor's hands, then in my own hands, cradled in my palms, lowered into a purifying fire, restoring balance to her defiled body.

But the doctor says it's medical waste. A biohazard.

"I don't understand why a part of my mother inside her body is a tumor, and outside her body it's a biohazard." My voice rises.

My mother's uterus is toxic waste, I say, the dregs from our bodies and the mine are the same poison from the same place. But her tumor will be disposed of and the gold mine will expand. Why can't he see this?

The doctor looks at me kindly. He has dealt with family members before. But what can a kind smile hide? Some women die on the operating table, never make it to join their sisters in Nurses Creek. I remember the stories of our own women, secretly sterilized in European operating rooms. *May all such doctors be dragged to Nurses Creek for their crimes against us.*

My mother's doctor stands his ground. His eyes are warm, but now his arms are folded across his chest. He looks down at his watch.

I might not be attached to keeping my mother's uterus, but something in our tangled life needs to be cut out, burned off.

Recovery Room

They've slotted her in three weeks ahead of schedule. Pacing back and forth in the hospital hallways crowded with machinery, it's hard for me not to imagine the wet lifting and sorting of innards, rearranging of parts, the two sides of my mother's stomach meeting each other again, stapled like pages in a book. Hours later the doctor comes to me down the hall to tell me she's in the recovery room. He says everything went well. They removed a tumor the size of a cantaloupe. *Thanks doctor. I will never eat cantaloupe again.* He tells me they got everything. *Did you get her anger?* I want to ask. *Did you get her shame?*

In the narrow hospital bed my mother looks like a child. She drifts in and out. "Keep it away," she says in a voice I can barely hear.

"What? Keep what away?"

"That juke."

"Mother, there's no dog in here."

"There is."

She sleeps again. Later, eyes clouded and barely open, she tells a fractured story of a new book and pencils and birds in the hedgerow. About a fresh morning path to school. "He set his dog on me," she whispers.

"Who? Who set his dog on you?"

"The man." Tears are leaking from the corners of her eyes. She turns her face to her pillow to dry them. "The man in town."

"What town? Where?"

"Worsley was it? By the Worsley Brook."

"Where, Mam? Where's the Worsley Brook?"

With great effort she waves her arm. "Over the bari panni."

"You mean England?"

She doesn't answer.

O Mam. You small helpless child, still walking that path to school all these years later. With a corner of the sheet I blot fresh tears from her face. She dozes off. When she half-opens her eyes, I brush her hair away from her face and ask about the man, about the dog.

"I don't know what you're talking about," she snaps, sitting up. "Stop bothering me with your idiotic stories and bring me a glass of water." I've put a pot of plastic orchids on the hospital tray but when she sees them she makes a face and turns away. "Fake," she says. "Like your marriage."

This is too much. She's too much. Too demanding, harsh, needy, cold. The list piles itself up as I stand to leave, and then I remember what I'd said to her. That I loved her. *Kamav tu.* How much I wanted to hear her say it back. I want to hear her say it even now. *Kamav tu, murri shey.*

Maybe she hates me with all her body. Maybe the cancer was the seat of her hate. A roof leak drains from the attic, crumbling the foundation, the mother house collapsing from the inside out.

Stories

In my mother's back yard, we sit in her two lawn chairs, looking over the tangle of raspberry bushes and dogwoods to the trees beyond.

"My womb," she says, cradling her stomach. "Your nest. You and me, inseparable all them months."

Are those tears at the edges of her eyes?

"There was no shame then."

She takes my hand and puts it on her stomach. I'm almost too angry and wound-up for this. Especially after yesterday. But I relax my hand, keeping it there. An uncomfortable intimacy, but I won't pull away.

"Nothing bad ever happened in them days," she says. "Just my body feeding yours, and you growing." We sit like that, my hand over the bandages and staples that hold her body together. I soften into her story. "It was the purest time. The only pure time."

The only pure time. This is it: our struggle. Her kind of purity is an overarching truth, acknowledged and respected, something from history, necessary for survival. A code embedded, the legacy of the Elders, the puri fowki. For me, though, purity is the orchid fen, my nights with Jack. My purity is a whispered *kamav tu,* morning water cupped in my hands, lifted to my face. All pure. All cleansing. My version of purity may not be hers. Purity, though, did not disappear after I was born. It is not finite. I reject my mother's notion and its stranglehold over me.

Before I can stop myself, I ask her again about the man and his dog.

"It's true," she whispers. "My daddus couldn't help me." I hate how she topples under these words. The walls of the mother house lie around us. I take her by the hand, lead her from the bricks and dust. Outside of this rubble, it's easier to separate the pure from the defiled. When she was a little girl, purity was stepping out to the cool morning, dew on the fields. It was her new schoolbook and her pencils and the birds in the hedgerows. Defiled was the man who set his dog on her as she walked to school, and her father, beaten by the man's son, unable to protect her. This defilement shaped her idea of purity forever.

"Look at the garden," she says, shaking her head, as if she's just wakened up. "What a mess."

"Should we walk a little? The doctors say you need to walk."

"No. I want to sit with you." She keeps my hand against her stomach. Then, out of the blue, she says, "I'm sorry. I know it was a long time ago. I didn't want to leave you. I really didn't." Here, again, comes the story of little Heron Galveston, how she went to care for him after his mother died.

You said it would be a month but a child can't measure a month.

Each breakfast was a year. Each supper another year. Each night stretched past the moon as I lay under the shards of light coming in Dalia Doroshenko's window.

She doesn't let go of my hand, but instead presses it harder against her. When we're laid bare and opened, buried remorse can't be held down.

A few minutes later she asks me to take her inside. When I bring her a bowl of soup, her face is raw with leftover tears.

At night I lie beside her in bed. I have a dream that doesn't feel like a dream: my mother is still sitting in the lawn chair, trying to make herself smaller than a stolen orchid root. She dissolves in shame.

A Child's Question

After I return from my shift at the greenhouse, I find my mother outside in her lawn chair again. "Remember when we came here?" she says. "To this town?"

I was ten years old when she put her finger on the map and said, *Look, shey. Here is a town named for red. This is where we belong.*

We came here, to our new home in Carminetown, on a warm day in July. We didn't settle in right away. We'd never settled in anywhere, even though we longed to; but longing had nothing to do with the real world.

Before we unpacked our suitcases and boxes, we went out walking. We kept to the small meadows and stands of trees at the back of the houses, and followed a narrow path that opened out to a place where sun refracted off the water and the air was dizzy and gold. *It's a fen,* said Mam. *An orchid fen.* I remember asking a child's question: I asked if we were home. If we could stay here and not move again ever.

We went to the orchid fen every Sunday the way other families went to church. Near the shore, our feet stirred the water and the light flashed off the wings of damselflies. We found dragon's mouth, white bog orchids, the showy yellow lady's slippers.

A fen without orchids is like a child without a mother, she said.

Who needs a church, she said, when we have the fen?

In the forested glade, we sat under the ironwood tree among the tall pink lady's slippers. It was then that we saw a single small white orchid. Rare, endangered, bone-clean as a vole's skull. Even as a child, I understood that sighting as a sign.

Now my mother has settled into her lawn chair, eyes closed. I think she might be sleeping, but then she says, "Everything that's happened since we came here —" She stirs, shifting her weight, cutting herself off with a sigh. "So much has changed." Her voice low and quiet, barely audible above the late afternoon hum of the garden.

I take her back to her room. She falls asleep immediately. When I leave her bedside, the light's slanting low. I go to the front door, and a pot of soup, still warm, sits on the porch. Blue chanterelle soup in Jack's blue enamel pot. I love him for this gift.

I bring a bowl of soup to my mother. She stirs in bed, eyeing the bowl in my hands.

"Look, Mam. Are you hungry? Here's some nice soup."

"Made by him? By that mush?"

"If you mean Jack, then yes."

While Mam's eating, I send him a text. I thank him, telling him she must like it because she has already started on her second bowl. With this offering he has reached out to me. I appreciate now that no gesture of his is conditional; he's not trying to announce or insert himself. In this moment I long for him, but he's there and I am here still.

Even in my gratitude, I don't know how to be with him. I don't know how to be without him. I want to see him across the kitchen table from me, wake up beside him in our bed. But I'm learning there are different loves. Separate, simultaneous. Jack-love, Mother-love. It's dizzying; if there are two, there must be more. Jack, how many loves does he have? The fen. Me. The guys at the Sylvanite. I don't know who or what else.

A week later I get a text. what's going on it's been a week. I don't text back.

> if u want to leave just say so
>
> > i dont want to leave
>
> then come home bring your mother
> with you

He says it's okay to be scared. When he says he knows I love my mother, I understand he means *my difficult mother* and he sees her in me too. I'm sorry, I'm sorry, I say. I'm sorry I've failed. I don't know how to be with you.

He says, no orchid u have not failed u dont need to be perfect for me u are perfect

The Move

My mother lets Jack take her arm.

"I don't like this," she says as they approach our door together. *Neither do I,* I think I hear him say. They're moving slowly, Jack watching each of her precarious steps.

"I don't like you," she says. "In fact, I hate you."

His quiet face doesn't register a thing. "We can turn around, JadeMarie," he says. "I'll take you home. Is that what you want?"

"You bastard," Mam says under her breath.

"JadeMarie," says Jack, turning toward her. "Who do we both love?"

She doesn't move. "Bastard," she says again.

They're at the top step. They come through the door.

"We're going to get along," says Jack. "Like it or not."

He lets her go ahead and she shuffles after me to the back room. I open her suitcase and begin putting things away. "Look, Mam," I say. I sound like a cheerleader. "You can see the gardens from your window."

"Get out my nightgown," she says. I help her undress, not looking at her naked body, the slowly healing scar across her stomach. She lies down and I pull up the sheet, tuck it around her. "This bed," she says, "is not like my bed."

"No."

She reaches out and takes my hand. "What will happen to me? To us?" she asks. Her question's a door, and we step through the distance between us. I kiss her forehead. She puts her hands on either side of my face and keeps it against hers. "Thank you," she says. I stay too long.

"Kamav tu," I say.

Finally, she asks me to go.

In the kitchen, Jack is at the stove. "Is she not eating?"

"No."

He puts out two bowls. We eat his week-old soup. He's closed to me, shoulders tight. I put down my spoon and push my bowl aside. I fold my hands on the table.

"Jack," I say. It's important to begin with his name. "This is not the way it's supposed to be."

"No?" says Jack, raising an eyebrow. "What way is it supposed to be?"

I'm pulled between Jack and my mother's need. A miserable tug-of-war. Can there be any other outcome but that he will want us both to leave after all? He'll be sick of us. When I don't answer, he pulls his chair closer to the table and hunches over his bowl. He eats furiously and tells me he's angry and he loves me and I wouldn't understand because I take the easy way out and pretend not to be here.

"What do you mean *'here?'*"

"Here. In this house. In this life."

Maybe Jack is not the man I knew him to be, and my vision of him in the fen was a mirage. But I, too, am not the person I used to be. Even in the short time of our marriage, we've morphed into new selves. Is that what marriage does? Makes shapeshifters of people who believe they belong together? Forces us to fit and refit to new ways of belonging?

I watch Jack's face, and the sighting from those years ago comes back to me: the lush scape of his body held by the tendrils and stems of the islet. I see through the tissues and bones to his beating core; not just the physicality of him, but the idea that such a man could exist. That day in the fen, his beauty was too real. Or my eyes were too dazzled. How long, in a marriage, can you be dazzled? After a time the trance slips into a kind of madness, or evaporates into thin air.

"What happened to our fen love?" I ask.

"That?" says Jack, faint smile at the corners of his mouth. "That's the beginning." This, now, is another stage, he says, his words a little less clipped. But he still can't look at me. We sit at the table, looking down at our empty bowls.

It's hard to feel comfort in this place that should be my home. I turn to the dark moving waters of Nurses Creek. A place where the panni raklies sing songs of a world neither here nor there. If I asked them about my life, I'd expect an answer I wouldn't want to hear.

Jack and I end up talking about nothing in particular. This is how it should be right now: light voices in the space between supper and bed. Later, we lie close under the night-blue sheets. I don't remember falling asleep.

Watching

In the kitchen, my mother watches Jack like a hawk. The way he scours surfaces, prepares food, his fervent cleanliness, he's like a Romany mush. My mother says nothing, but I think he's passing the test.

"He reminds me of little Heron," she says. "How I imagine Heron all grown up." Heron, whose father had a house burned down with three people inside. I don't say this. It would only start an argument.

Pie 2

Jack sits back, chair angled against the wall, hands on his stomach. We've been eating his moose stew from the freezer. "You're still here," he says. His voice brings me back to myself. To the yellow walls, the evening light. When I look at him across the table, I see a softness in his shoulders, his mouth, his beautiful long limbs. His body as open as it was in our first days.

The pie between us is saskatoon berry, the last of the season from the tree in the garden. I made it an hour ago, the ritual of pastry and berries and sugar anchoring the day. The stirring of the fruit, the rolling of the crust, each motion another root into this house, into the garden. When the ritual is over and consecrated with the heat of the oven, I cut one piece, slide it to his side of the table, lift the fork to his mouth. I cut another piece, and we feed each other. The dark sweetness of the berries fills our mouths and stains our lips. Nothing else matters.

I cut a slice for my mother. No light shines from under her door. She must be asleep. I leave the plate on the hall table.

In our bed, Jack holds himself over me. I can't see him in the dark. He's like a shadow with no source. All I need is this: his generous warmth to fold me in.

He says again, "You're still here."

In the morning he takes the remains of the pie to work. Wrapped in aluminum foil, it travels with him into the cage and down the shaft.

◆

After supper, Jack again angles his chair against the wall. His sated look from last night is gone. My mother watches.

"So," he says, sitting forward, closed fists on the table. "We've got problems."

Problems. Really, Jack? Last night was not enough? The still-vivid memory of last night's pleasure, last night's comfort collapses around me.

Again he says, "problems."

"Here?"

Jack frowns. "No, no. Nothing like that."

Mam gets up from the table. "I'm going to bed," she says.

Problems

Two men from the mine are in hospital with silicosis. In the tunnels, the miners who are not yet sick breathe diesel fumes, silica, dust. From frog life, moss life, lily life to dust. When I close my eyes I can see the dust seep from the earth, hang over Jack, over the fen. This is the problem at the root, but new problems sprout all around us. After three failed attempts, Jack meets with the managers to discuss working conditions. The managers look through him.

Anyone wanna bet the air's above legal limits, says Jack.

Send inspectors, say the managers.

Inspectors paid by Galveston?

In the underground cafeteria, the miners eat their lunch. In the hall outside, the managers talk to the supervisors. Sexsmith, the supervisor for Jack's shift, comes into the cafeteria and says, *Get back to work.*

The miners say, *We aren't finished.*

Young Cyril Lepke, he doesn't get up. He's eating his sandwich. Beef brisket with barbecue sauce. *Lepke,* warns Sexsmith, standing over him.

Cyril Lepke chews. He smiles at Sexsmith around his mouthful of brisket. Before he's finished, he opens his lunchbox and takes out a second sandwich, looks up at the clock.

We got five more minutes, he says, and unwraps the second sandwich. *This one's ham,* he says. *Want a bite?* He offers the sandwich.

Sexsmith's jaw tightens.

What's your problem? says Cyril. *You don't like ham sandwiches?* He chews loudly. Two minutes after the hour he's still chewing.

The older miners love Lepke. He's like their spiky teenage kid. Lepke, with his mullet and hockey sweaters and missing front tooth. After this first incident with the sandwich, Cyril taunts Sexsmith every shift. He sings when Sexsmith walks by.

The working class can kiss my ass
I've got the boss's job at last.

Every day Cyril eats his lunch two minutes past the hour.

Buffalo wings today, he says, waving a wing at Sexsmith.

There's no rushing pulled pork, licking his lips.

Ordinary old salami, he says, opening the wrapping for Sexsmith to see. *But at least I got Mom's date squares she made last night. Better than Irene Slepchik's, but don't tell auntie Irene.* He leans in to Sexsmith. "*Secret ingredient's the cricket powder Mom grinds by hand in her kitchen. For the protein, you know.*"

Scrappy fatherless Lepke and his daily lingering lunch are the last straw. The bosses dock his pay. The next day, Lepke juts his jaw at Sexsmith — an angle as hard as a hockey stick. That's the end for Sexsmith and his short fuse. He punches Lepke, who reels back and crashes into the table behind him.

Finishing Line

Ten men are crammed around the kitchen table, eating Jack's moose stew. Jack is different around the men. He has a swaggering energy, walks with his legs wide, sits with his elbows on the table. He smells different. A meaty, male stench, like horse or bull. Is this the Jack he wears out in the world? Or is it the real Jack, the one I've failed to see?

Cyril Lepke lifts his shirt to show the bruise across his ribs. He's white as cotton grass except for the heavy blue of the bruise, its yellow edges. Then he turns to show the deeper bruise on his back.

"From where I landed," he laughs.

Somebody — Sexsmith likely, probably others — is naming names around the mine, so the men start their own list. The men at our kitchen table have names for Sexsmith. *Prick* is the least offensive.

We don't sleep after the men have gone. The kitchen table rocks under us. I breathe the stale air from Jack's skin. The smell of wild game love. Of metal and minerals and mud. I feel the orchid fen all around us, and the bed in the next room, our collapsing marriage bed floats over the watery surface. Jack's holding back from a finishing line. It's frightening, this moment before finality.

JadeMarie and the Moon

I take my mother's empty suitcase back to her house and pack a second nightgown, socks, t-shirts, skirts, jeans. A new toothbrush, a new hairbrush. Her sewing machine, her box of needles and thread.

"What's going on?" she says, when she sees the suitcase.

"I'm just bringing more of your things."

"Am I really moving in? Is this it?"

"Yes."

In her new bedroom, my mother sits with the curtains open to the night, face pressed against the window. The moon is almost full. Tomorrow or the next day it will be called the Sturgeon Moon, she says, named for the times when the sturgeon of the Great Lakes were plentiful. "She's so close," says Mam. "I want to touch her." The moon is outsized tonight, a silver disc looming over the trees.

"You're a miner," she says, turning to Jack, who is standing at the door. "What do miners think of the moon?"

Before he can open his mouth to answer, she has moved on to Galveston. She says, almost spitting her words, that when Galveston looks at the moon, he doesn't see the cycles of the months or the tides. He only sees planted flags and digging machines after the mines of the earth are emptied out. I think the panni raklies would agree with her; there's a terrifying expansiveness to the idea of them singing about the moon's beauty when they're so awash in the dead green waters. Galveston doesn't care about the deep underground rivers and caves where life hides. His roots are unraveling metal threads, razor-edged, drenched with arsenic, cyanide, slicing through the tendrils of grasses and orchids. His footprints are caked with mercury.

Then Mam drags Heron into it. "Poor Heron," she says. "It's his father and that company of his that are the problem."

◆

When my mother's second suitcase is unpacked, Jack comes home with a cardboard box. From this box, my mother lifts a sketchbook, pencils, a pair of binoculars.

"Wow," she says, trying not to look delighted. "What am I supposed to do with this?"

"You can draw the moon," says Jack, "if you want." He ducks out of the room, leaving her with these gifts.

"O shey," she says, bringing her hands to her face. "I never dreamed anybody would do such a thing for me. Or that I'd be deserving of it."

She lifts the binoculars and looks at the moon, turning the dial to adjust the focus.

"It's like seeing our moon from the fen. It was just us and the moon. Do you remember? And now here she is, up close. I see things here that I never thought possible. Dark and light, jagged edges, silver and not-silver."

She draws page after page of lunar maps. Then she draws herself beside the moon, her hair longer and darker than it really is, and a flowered diklo around it. She signs her drawing: *JadeMarie and the Moon.*

Learning

"Thank you, Jack."

"You're welcome."

"It was kind of you. It made me feel better. Really."

"I'm glad."

When she leaves the kitchen, Jack says, "I'm learning."

My mother, too, is learning. I'm learning. Together we learn.

Quiet

In the days that follow, Cyril Lepke lodges a complaint against Sexsmith. Two men appear on his way home from the Sylvanite Hotel. They rough him up. Bruise upon bruise upon bruise. Three more miners are cornered and beaten by other men. Those men can't be identified. It's always dark, and their faces are covered, but their stance — the ugly way they hold their bodies over the bruised and bleeding miners — could only have been learned from Sexsmith or others like him.

The guys begin going to and from work in twos and threes. Jack and Sexsmith have a shouting match in the cafeteria. Later, coming out of the Sylvanite, three men swarm Jack from behind. He fights back. He doesn't know these men; they aren't from around here. Jack comes home with a swollen cheekbone, a black eye.

"It's okay," he says, turning away when I bring a cool cloth to his face. "Shit happens. You gotta move on."

Then it all goes quiet, like a storm holding its breath.

Messaging

                                        hey

r u there

                                        yes

sorry missed supper

                    its okay leftovers here

did your mam eat

      yes and she came into the kitchen on
                                  her own

lol

      says she likes your moose stew even if
                it did come from the freezer

lol

        and your mushroom soup with the
              sourdough rye I just made

im gonna win her over yet

      never thought it was possible but yes

ill lure her with food its my next job

                                        lol

we're at macs back around ten

The Orchid as Oracle

The mycorrhizal fungus seeks nourishment without which it faces starvation. Its need is met only with the dust-seed of the orchid in the fen, on the shore, or in the leaf-mold and rot of the old growth forest above the marshy realm.

Each recognizing the other, seed and fungus embrace. They are consumed by urgency: for the orchid, sustenance; for the fungus, a home (Stymus, Grey 2022, 47).

The fungus digests earth-nutrients for the orchid, allowing the fleshy roots and corms to shoot forth and spread; it is in these roots and corms that the nutrients are stored.

The orchid welcomes the fungus into its heart. Both rejoice when the corms form leaves, and ultimately new orchids, and in this way the orchid sends forth its young to inhabit fresh domains (Hill, Laakso 2013, 119). Host and guest in symbiosis, a permanent embrace (Field, Trace et al. 2017, 79).

The flower opens: three orgasmic spiraling sepals, three top petals, a lower flared lip awaiting the wasp, the moth, the bee.

An orchid may be endangered. It seeks sister-orchids but remains isolated, nourished only by its guest. The endangered orchid cannot be *killed, harmed, harassed, captured or taken, and its habitat cannot be damaged or destroyed* (Committee on the Status of Species at Risk in Ontario 2007).

If the fungus fades, so does the orchid, but not before singing a lament of imbalance in the body politic. For the scientist, the declining orchid is an oracle. A bio-indicator. Its absence is a warning about the health of the ecosystem in which it grows (Van Kouverden and Marsh 1953, 65).

References

Committee on the Status of Species at Risk in Ontario. *Policy Guidance on Harm and Harass Under the Endangered Species Act.* 2007. https://www.ontario.ca/page/policy-guidance-harm-and-harass-under-endangered-species-act#section-4.

Hill, Laakso. 2013. *Orchid Colonization.* Coburn and Farrow.

Field, Trace et al. 2024. "The Northern Orchid Fen." *Orchidaceae Botanica* 100(13): 71–90.

Stymus and Grey. 2022. *Symbiosis and Gratification in Orchid-Mycorrhizal Communion.* Jansons, Fugler and Smith.

Van Kouverden and Marsh. 1953. *The Orchid as Oracle.* Fenn and Greenside.

Love Twelve Times

Iris Blythe tells me there's a meeting at the town hall about the new gold mine. I don't want to think about the mine, or about the fen and the death of the fen. Iris is going for the free food. Also she wants to see the city people, the mine's lawyers and executives who come from who knows where. She wants to eat sandwiches and pastries and listen to how they talk, see how they dress. She calls them "cidiots."

The town hall is packed. A woman we don't know greets each person at the door. "Welcome," she says. "Welcome, folks." Her eyes and her smile don't match.

I smell the metal chairs and coffee and tuna salad sandwiches and the polish on the cracked linoleum floor. Somewhere under this smell lies the distant miasma of gouged earth, chemical soup, noxious tailings. I can't tell if these are real, or if they're the smells of the future.

The woman gestures at the coffee urn. She hasn't stopped smiling. "Hi there, dear," she says to Iris, who makes a beeline for the food table.

"Tuna," says Iris, stacking sandwiches on her palm. I hide from Iris in a group of newcomers, but I can't hide from Primrose Kowalski, who's milling through the crowd with Queenie, the slip-pery nurse from Food World. Primrose is holding onto Queenie's arm like her life depends on it, but when she sees me, she smiles. I smile back, willing her to stay away. I can't tell her what I know: *I see your dead sister at the river with the panni raklies.* My sight goes suddenly dark and I'm swallowing panic. All I want is to go home and wait for Jack.

When my eyes clear, Primrose and Queenie have turned away, and are sitting with Rose, who waves at me from her place beside her aunt. Now Irene Slepchik and Dalia Doroshenko, Mrs. Doherty and other women from our street have taken up a row behind me. Are they all here for the city clothes and the free food?

A man and woman sit behind a table at the front of the hall. They're upright, uncomfortable, important, shining hair arranged as if lowered onto their heads. In front of them, the binders and sheaves of paper are a shield between themselves and the people of the town. Calling these people presenters, the mayor introduces them. When the presenters stand at the podium, looking down at us, they thank us for being a part of "a community conversation." Then they shuffle awkwardly through a land acknowledgement, sliding a package of tobacco to the edge of their table.

"It's an offering," they say loudly, craning their necks at Marjorie Commanda and the Elders.

The presentation is friendly and bright, with colored maps and graphs, complicated diagrams stretching across the wall behind them: beavers, damselflies, backhoes, orchids, streams, towers, a woman smiling at a gold wedding ring on her finger.

Before the presentation is finished, Lennie Pomerantz says, "This is bullshit," and leaves. A grumble moves through the rows.

"Call me Mallory," says the first presenter, as if remembering her manners. Mallory smiles out at the room.

I turn to look at Iris. She nods, excited, and gives Mallory's city clothes a thumbs-up.

"We love this town and its people," Mallory says. She wets her lips with a flick of her tongue. "The forests, we love your forests.

And your beautiful lakes and rivers." Coral-red lipstick lines her dry mouth. Faint sweat marks the peachy blouse.

"We're here," she says, licking her lips again, "because we'd love to hear your ideas."

Mallory says "love" twelve times.

Behind me Irene Slepchik yells, "Where's Orchid Lake?" Everybody turns to look at her. She stabs her finger at the power-point photograph on the wall. I'm delighted by her glued-on red nails — I've never seen fake nails on her before. Five red switch-blades stabbing at the air. "How come we don't see Orchid Lake in them pictures?"

The other presenter, who calls himself Damien, says things like *environmental impact assessment*, and *boosting community engagement*. "Hang on, dear," he says. "We'll get there."

But "dear" has hit a nerve. Irene jumps up. She shakes her cane in the air. "Orchid Lake, you cidiot," she yells. People laugh. This is the beginning of the end for Damien. He tries for a small recovery, shuffling some papers in front of him, dropping them on the floor.

Orchid Lake will be the new home of the runoff, he says finally, pointing to bulrushes around a square pond with a back-drop of trucks, buildings, chain link fences. "Wetlands are natural filtration systems. The bulrushes and other aquatic plant life will remove a wide array of contaminants," he recites. "Why, we'll leave your lake cleaner than it is now. Guaranteed." His voice is too bright. "The new Orchid Lake lagoon will house the runoff from gold production."

"That don't look like no runoff," says Irene, wagging her fingers at the crystalline waters of the lagoon.

"It'll be safe," says Damien. "Trust me."

"What's in your runoff anyways?" That's Iris Blythe. For Iris, and for most of the audience in the hall, watching the city people flounder is the best entertainment. Maybe she's lost interest in city fashion.

"Just the chemicals that help us make the gold," says Damien.

Somebody in the back yells, *"Just. Just* the chemicals."

The high school science teacher stands. "Heavy metals, cyanide, arsenic …"

"… the gold that will bring jobs and prosperity to your community." Damien is trying to talk over the teacher, who has continued to recite the complicated names of gold mining contaminants.

The fen's tugging at me. The lilies, the orchids, the moving water. I can smell them. Silence isn't an option. I didn't plan to, but I have to stand up. I have to speak. "Have you been to Orchid Lake? Have you been to the orchid fen?"

Damien and Mallory look at each other. Damien leans toward her and lowers his voice. "What's a fen?" he says.

Fish

When Marjorie Commanda stands, Damien's hands tighten on the edges of his binder. "Your gold mine," she says, "will use twenty bodies of water inhabited by fish."

"That's right," says Damien, dry mouth clicking into his microphone. Now he's in free fall.

"We eat those fish," she says.

"Okaaay," says Damien.

"Where are those fish going to go?" Marjorie Commanda waits.

"Hang on there," Damien says. He's racing through his slides, a sequence of colors, words, numbers, pie charts, arrows, diagrams flashing across the wall behind him. Then a distant mine shaft, in the foreground a pink-skinned family eating sandwiches at a picnic table. "We'll get to your fish."

"Patiently hanging on here," says Marjorie Commanda, smiling.

"Nearly there," says Damien.

Now a black bear cub eating dandelions. Yellow bright against the black fur.

"Awww," says Mallory. She turns to the audience with her hand on her heart.

Damien stops at a gathering of fish snouting through greenish-grey water. It's cloudy; mud has been disturbed.

"Those aren't our fish," says Marjorie Commanda. "Those are catfish."

Damien's mouth opens and shuts.

"Specifically, channel catfish," she says, "found in the southern United States. Our fish are lake trout, bass, yellow perch and so on."

Damien swallows hard.

"Where do you suggest we find new fish if these are sacrificed for your gold mine?" Some people at the back start clapping. Damien and Mallory are looking at each other, faces pale and shining under layers of bronzer. Marjorie Commanda sits perched on the edge of her seat, ready to stand again.

"We're glad you asked that question," says Mallory. She plucks at her blouse. "We're here to work together. To find —" She coughs. "— find new places for your fish. We have sustainable mining practices. Very robust mining practices," she says, nodding. "Very."

She no longer says *love*.

"Yes. It's in our plan. To find new places for your fish."

"So, no real answer then," says Marjorie Commanda.

"Yay, Auntie," calls Rose.

Irene Slepchik starts down the aisle, stabbing her cane into the floor. She swears at the presenters. I've never heard her swear. A security guard closes in on her, takes her arm.

"Who the hell are you?" says Irene, yanking her arm away. "You prick," she adds, clawing at his eye with her gloriously fake nails. "Don't you be touching me." Iris Blythe comes up from behind. She hits the man with her purse. Two more women shove him off and he shoves back. Iris Blythe is knocked to the floor. Everything falls apart.

Waiting

On the way home I text Jack, Omg u wont believe what just happened

Jack doesn't answer.

The house is dark. I go out to the garden, then over to Nurses Creek, and don't find him. The panni raklies are further upstream by the shore. One of them whose face I don't know, whose face is too far gone to know, chants a slow dirge about explorations being back on. I text him again, saying the panni raklies are predicting that the mine's going ahead. Does he know anything? Anything at all? Jack doesn't answer. I call out over the water. "Have you seen him? Have you seen my Jack?"

The house is still dark when I get home, the kitchen clock glowing 10:32. Jack isn't here. I don't think to get into my nightgown. At 10:45 I'm texting again. I call, text, call, text, call. I thumb through my contacts, trying anyone who might have seen him, waking my neighbors in their beds. At eleven I reach Mac McCarthy's daughter. "Jack? He left our place an hour ago," she says. "Maybe he went by the Sylvanite," she offers.

Eleven-thirty. Midnight. Two a.m. I keep texting. I call. I don't dare go outside. What if he comes, and I'm not here? I'll have to act as if everything's normal. *I'll put on my nightgown, get into bed, sit up when I hear your footsteps outside the bedroom door, feel you nudge me, hear you say it's okay, go back to sleep, but I wake up anyway, so glad to feel your body against mine.*

"Jack," I shout into the phone, "Jack."

At three in the morning he still isn't here. I run outside, run back to Nurses Creek. *Where are you? I can't lose you. Come back.* The panni raklies are in the river and I silently beg them for reassurance. For help. Anything. They float against the shore, rise in the shallows, bones shining through the remnants of their skin. I smell the rot. Why are their faces so bleak, when all I want from them is comfort? *Revenge. They're imagining revenge.* I see it in what remains of their eyes.

Quick. Hold the dread at bay.

But now everything's running together.

Jack on the islet in the fen, Jack at the kitchen table (he'll be there now, eating his cold moose stew), Jack nuzzling my neck in the garden, in our bed. But then there's Jack in his truck, driving too fast, Jack in the gaze of the panni raklies, their grim gaze, and my screaming doesn't work. No one can hear it. It's Jack who's screaming.

Irene finds me in the street.

"Oh, my baby," she says. "Oh, my girl." She puts her arms around me, warm as bread. She steers me back to our house. As we walk, she hollers, "Jack! Jack Bachinski!"

My mother's at the front door. "What the hell's going on?"

She brings me a blanket, swaddles my bones, which seem to have gotten loose inside my skin. I can't hear her or can't make sense of her, but Irene Slepchik is talking frantically. She has lost the red nail from one of her fingers and I can't take my eyes off the film of glue on her nail bed like peeling skin.

Mam's hand — soft, thick-fingered — puts a cup of tea on the table in front of me. She lifts the cup to my mouth because my arms won't move and my body can only shiver. Part of me is held tight inside the blanket. The rest of me is running through the streets.

Jack, Jack.

Irene hovers, patting my shoulder. "How can I help?"

"It's okay," says Mam. "Thank you."

I hear Irene going out the door and my mother moving around the kitchen. The sound of water boiling, of more tea poured into the cup, the rattle of the cup in the saucer. Then there are arms around me again, holding me together. My mother says, "It'll be okay. They'll find him."

Time swells and contracts. The hands on the kitchen clock barely move. They jump forward whole millennia.

Did I fall asleep? The sun is bright in the window and a voice in the kitchen — no, a voice beside me, from a body I can't see behind the slanting light — tells me that Jack's truck has been found. It's at the bottom of a ravine outside town. This voice, which seems to belong to a policeman, talks loud and slow, as if I'm a child.

"Alive. Your husband is alive."

He says Jack's lucky. He should have been dead. But isn't. There are more words I don't understand. Other voices are here too, ones I know. Mac McCarthy. Rose. Irene Slepchik again. My mother makes me drink tea and eat a piece of toast.

Shroud

A long shape. A shroud of skin, red, purple, shining, cracking, rising, falling. Frantic effort in the heave and drop and heave of breath. A hand or something like a hand. I reach for whatever it is. Yes, it's a hand. A shape I understand by touch rather than sight. It's the wrong color, the wrong texture, but I know it's the hand that picked the mushrooms, stirred the soup, held me in so many ways. Such pleasure from this hand.

A tube connects the ruined weeping hand of my husband to a transparent bag. A solution fills the bag suspended from a stand. I count the steady drip, drip, drip from the bag into the tube. Now I know the quality of this love, different from all others, when at any second he could leave me. One small last breath and then gone where I can't follow. Gone.

Jack, Jack.

Even in this hospital room I'm calling for him, my whole body calling into the stale air, calling over the fen, over the town, the forests and rivers. In this moment I love him more for fear of losing him. I love him without words. No words but his name.

There are too many machines around the shroud. Wet red bandages. A tube disappearing into a hole. Gurgling, a wet gasp. More snaking tubes connecting the shroud to more machines. Sssssclick. Sssssclick. Sssssclick. I want to kiss the hole that might be a mouth.

Brush Your Hair

You look in the mirror. Now you look in the mirror. You see your face, the orchid face with its swollen lip, pulling back like dark pools of brackish water. Your face fades into darkness, or moves out of the frame. It's hard to tell which. You're trying to brush your hair. You brush your hair because Mam says, *brush your hair.* The brush peels your scalp away.

No. That's Jack you're thinking about.

His peeled scalp, his segmented body. Broken into parts in places that are not logical. A logical break is at the knee, ankle, shoulder, arm, neck. A break happens where the parts naturally join, and can be mended. But Jack's crushed like a beetle in the fen. His wounds are mokkadi. His body defiled.

Look at you. You're whole. A whole person. But are you whole, with the part that is Jack cut away? Jack a ghost limb, no longer attached. But you still feel him. You feel him in the garden, at the kitchen table, in bed. You palpate your head, chest, stomach. You palpate the cradle of your pumping heart.

Brush your hair, Mam calls.

At least do that one thing. The one thing that keeps you in this world. Tomorrow you can do more. Tomorrow you can brush your teeth. But for today, brush your hair.

Brake Line

"They cut the goddamned brake line," says Lennie Pomerantz. A tray of date squares, brought by Cyril Lepke's mother, sits on the table. "And they loosened his wheel nuts. You know who I'm talking about," Lennie says.

Mrs. Lepke's date squares are dry, with a thin filling. Crumbling on our best plate. Lennie Pomerantz reaches his hand toward the plate of date squares, and soon he has eaten three. He takes sips of tea between mouthfuls. Would it matter if he ate them all? Or should I save some for the panni raklies? With their prophetic vision, do they already know what has happened, or what will happen? If I bribe them with date squares will they tell me? Panni raklies don't eat, but they do like a sacrifice.

"Galvestons," says Lennie Pomerantz, chewing around the name everyone had already said to themselves. Crumbs fall onto the front of his shirt.

"Jack likes dates squares," I say. "I'm not very good at date squares but Irene Slepchik is."

My mother looks at me. "Hush, shey," she says. "We don't need to worry about date squares."

Lennie Pomerantz chews. He swallows thickly.

I lift the cup. "The crust always falls apart on me." I put the cup down. Falls apart. The crust of skin over the wound. All of Jack a wound. "Is Jack alive?" I ask.

Mam brings the cup to my lips. She whispers that I should not eat the date squares. They're filled with cricket powder and were made in a mokkadi kitchen. "The Lepkes' cat walks across the table," she says, quietly in my ear. "Licks the mixing bowls."

Mac McCarthy sits down beside me at the table. "Who can eat date squares at a time like this?" He makes a fist and punches the air. Later he eats two date squares. "So they loosened his wheel nuts and cut the brake line, did they?" he says, sitting back, folding his giant arms across his chest. "They're gonna pay for this."

Somewhere Inside

He's somewhere inside there. "Jack," I call. "Jack."

Jack's hand moves.

When the doctor arrives, he says terrible things in a voice too loud for such violence. Things I could barely whisper. It's hard to hear Jack's breathing over these words I don't want to hear. *Multiple breaks. Rib piercing right lung. Head trauma.* Then he says: "Toronto." They are transferring Jack to Toronto. Taking him away from me.

The next morning Jack's hand slips from mine as they load him into the ambulance like a package to be delivered. Who will receive such a delivery? I want them to know his name. To know that he is a cook, a worker, a husband, a lover. A man who knows the fen, who tries his best to like my mother. A man with unread-able eyes, who leaves me drained at night, who makes gardens, who drinks with his buddies, who drives too fast. I want them to know that he's Jack inside the wet papery wrapping of skin, yellow and grey now, the red soaked bandages. That he's more than the hole where his mouth should be, the open hole and the tube bringing the air into his lungs.

"Tell them his name," I call to the driver. "His name is Jack Bachinski." Without a word, the driver shuts the door and the ambulance moves slowly out of the parking lot. It disappears around the corner.

Eyes

Rose gives me a strawberry made of beads. It's sewn onto a strawberry-shaped piece of moose hide. She made it for Jack and me, and when I run my fingers over the beads, thinking of the hours she held the hide and beads and thread in her hands, I feel her love for us. She slept last night in the living room, and in the morning helps me pack my suitcase, setting aside a green dress for my trip. Green to remind me of the fen, she says. She doesn't know how grateful I am, and when I try to tell her, I'm saying thank you, again, for her beautiful strawberry.

Irene Slepchik sits with me in the bus station. She holds my hand and says *Don't worry, everything's gonna be fine, my girl.* She no longer has the red claws. Her fingernails are short and clean. Her hands are clean. She lists the ways in which she'll care for my mother. At least she does not have a cat that will lick the dishes or walk on the kitchen counter while she cooks.

As the bus leaves, she waves with her whole arm.

Seven hours later, I sit beside Jack in the hospital. I can't remember which one. There are many hospitals along both sides of this wide street with cars that flow and churn like water. But the name of the hospital isn't important. That I recognize it is suffi-cient. I follow blue painted feet on the floor, stepping within the outline of each foot. They guide me through the wide doors, across the lobby into the elevator. I count twenty-nine steps to Jack's door.

Two nurses are turning him from one side to the other as I come into the room with its blinking, beeping machines, its window overlooking the city. "Jack," says one of the nurses, looking up with a smile. "Guess who's here to see you?" She comes close, and in a low whisper tells me he's in an induced coma. "But it's important to keep talking to him as you'd normally do."

They have turned him away from me, so I talk to his back, telling him about Rose's beaded strawberry. About the continuing date square battle: Mrs. Lepke's versus Irene Slepchik's. About the fen. "The water lilies are still blooming, their petals have started to get ragged, and the lily pads are curling, and some of them are yellow at the edges, Jack. Jack." The words leave my mouth, ghost words dispersing in the air.

Much later the nurses come back.

"Lucky you," they tell him. "Look at your beautiful wife. We're turning you over now, so you can see her. Look, Jack. What a gorgeous green dress she's wearing."

They turn Jack again so he faces me. He doesn't look like Jack. His features are crushed — eyes, nose, jaw colliding with each other. I don't know what's inside this shroud of bandages. What if he's someone else, an imposter they've wrapped and tucked into this bed so I'll be deceived into thinking he's alive?

This time I remember my words. *Tailings, birch grove, hands warmed on a bowl of moose stew, bodies warmed together.* I say *kamav tu.* An eyelid flutters like a torn wing, and opens. Jack's grey-green eye.

"It's you," I say to him. "Do you see me? Do you see Orchid who loves you?" I hold Rose's strawberry before his eyes. "Look, Jack. Look what Rose made for us."

I stay in a spare room in Irene Slepchik's niece's apartment. I go out in the morning and return at night. I don't remember much about the apartment or the room, even when I've left it only minutes before. All I have and all I am is funneled into Jack. The day I leave for Carminetown, I can't stop imagining Jack's two eyes, open, the color of fen water before rain.

On my first morning back home, I turn to the empty space beside me in bed and think of the greenhouse. Of the orchids. They'll need me. I say their names. *Pansy orchid. Slipper orchid. Vanilla planifolia. Moth orchid. Cattleya.*

But as I'm getting dressed, Iris Blythe comes to the front door, her face blotched and red. "We been fired," she says.

Dead Things

Up to my waist in water, I shiver as my nightgown floats around me. This is not real. It's a dream. No, the dark shapes rising are real, and closing in. I call to them but my voice shakes. They smell of dead fish. There is no breath coming from their open mouths. With their bodies they tell me to look at the river.

A small open vein of the earth, fit only for the dead, they say. *No life grows here. It's a snuff film. We should know: we remember our past living breathing selves, our bloody deaths. We are Mother Earth wiped out. Mullered. Destroyed.*

Sometimes we see him back there at night, walking across the tailings. We can't reach him. He doesn't come to the river. It's nothing to him. Where are the water plants? Where are the fish? His people did this. That's what they know.

The panni raklies are pressing close now, with their death-stink and their slippery melting skin. *Gord Kowalski. Coral Kowalski. The Galvestons, they tried to get Jack. No accident, that. Who do you think cut his brake line? Paid some desperate man to cut a brake line.*

My stomach rises and I stumble through the shallows.

Let him drink the poison from his river. Let him swim in it.

"Who?" I ask, although I already know. "Who?"

Heron Galveston. The panni raklies tell me I'll deliver him. They don't ask. *You'll bring him to us.* I remember Dalia

Doroshenko and her warning. *Them rusalkas, them river spirits, they want you for something.* They're still singing *bring him, bring him,* when one dissolving figure emerges from the group. It takes great effort for Coral Kowalski to pull her body back together. She's panting her river rot in my face.

"What about Jack?" I ask.

"Jack will be fine."

"How can you say that?"

"Relax," says Coral, smiling. "We've got Jack covered."

"What do you mean *covered?*" This terrifies me.

Coral tilts her head, and a long strand of algae drips from her hair. "Just what I say."

This is real. I'm dreaming. None of this is real.

"It's real," says Coral, as if I'd spoken aloud. "Things are gonna happen."

"What things?"

Coral grins. "Big things."

Then they're gone. Like that. Only the smell of them remains.

Sylvanite Sylvanite

Jack is in the hospital and my mother is sick again. I am stretched thin between them. She gets worse in the night, her fever blazing. A red line sneaks along her incision, and I want to scream at her *why are you always sick.*

"The pain," she whispers.

My own pain sits inside me like a nest of knives. *Mother, cancer, Jack, the panni raklies, the fen, and now again my mother. Always mother, mother, mother.*

I tell myself, *shut up, just shut up for once, this is not the time.*

I still somehow manage to take charge. I call an ambulance. At the hospital they admit her, and it's dark when I leave her room. The streets are like paths through another town, disturbed in the way of a dream. Everything's too quiet. Emptied out, hollow, except for a few men wheeling out the door of the Sylvanite. I'm in the middle of the street below the blinking lights: *Sylvanite Hotel, Sylvanite Hotel.* They change from red to white and back to red again.

A car slams on its brakes, the driver yelling, someone else screaming. I'm face down on the sidewalk. I turn my head. When my eyes clear, the lights of the Sylvanite Hotel have gone out.

The Rescue

A man puts his arm around me and lifts me to my feet.

"Where do you live?" he asks.

Where do I live?

He looks down at me. "You're in distress," he says.

"Yes."

"I don't mean to upset you," he says.

He's beside me, holding my arm. I see the streets as if under water or through rippled glass. Is this how it is for the panni raklies? A world changed by death. Even when you return to a place you know, you're not the same person in it. I'm not the same. Who belongs to this name Orchid Lovell? The stranger leads me through dark streets behind the houses, over a rose-tangled path. I let myself be guided. He limps slightly, as if from an old injury, but his movements are otherwise careful, studied, lithe.

"This way?" the stranger says. "This house here?"

"Yes."

He takes off his shoes at the door, leaving the outside outside, honoring the inside, knowing the difference. Cleanliness and purity against the dirt of the world. No defiled thing, no mokkadi thing in the house. Mam would approve, I think.

But what am I thinking? He's a stranger. A stranger should not be in my house. When I look at him more closely, I realize there is something familiar about this dark hair falling over his forehead, sharp nose, smooth skin. He puts on the kettle and makes tea, moving around the kitchen as if he knows it, owns it. *A man I don't know is making me tea.* He bends to peer into the fridge. "Cream? Sugar?"

"No."

The tea pouring into my cup. A small trickling river. His narrow white hand holding the spoon. Gold signet ring on his finger. The spoon clinking.

"Stirring helps cool it down," he says, as if I am a child. He says other things, and like a child I am calmed by the sound of this voice in the night, a dark voice that says nothing in particular. The steam is still rising from the tea when he reaches across the table for my hand, and I can smell some kind of perfume, sweetish, probably from Europe, probably worth more than two months of my wages.

"I'm sorry for whatever it is you're going through," he says. As I sip the tea, he tells me he saw me outside the Sylvanite, saw my face — a soft, good face, he says — and felt as if he knew me. I reminded him of someone he'd known long ago. He had to help. When we finish our tea he washes the cups and saucers and dries them as if someone, once, had taught him the proper way.

"I'll leave you now," he says. He puts his shoes on at the door. Fine leather, polished, the color of oxblood. I close the door behind him and watch him leave. From the front window I look out at the street lights, at the long, shuddering shadows of trees.

In the morning I rewash the two cups and two saucers left by the sink, and I know that yes, I'd brought a stranger into our house. A kind stranger who cared about me. About Jack. A man who made ordinary kitchen sounds and who spoke to me in a low voice.

Sorry

At the hospital, Mam asks about Jack. "How is he?"

"Alive."

She's connected to a drip. "Antibiotics," she says, looking toward the window.

"How are you?"

"A bit better."

The sun angles across her bed. In the hall, a gurney trundles past the door, wheels screeching. Her hand smooths the sheet, pats at the fabric bunched around her middle. Her other hand reaches for mine. "About Jack," says Mam. "I'm sorry."

Only once before has she said she's sorry. It's got to be hard for her.

"I may be a wreck but I know what's going on," she says. With the fen ripped out for a tailings pond we'll have nowhere to go, she says. Rivers will flow upstream. Frogs will grow many legs, or float white-bellied in the waters. Fish will swim upside down. Arsenic instead of blood will flow through our veins. This is what awaits us.

"Mam," I say, "it's the painkillers making you talk this way." But I know it isn't. I know she's right.

"No, murri shey, it's the future. The fen, our fen, she's like a mother. She gave us clean air and beauty and medicines. She'll be gone, gone to us, and we'll have no new fen to go to."

Texting

i know you cant answer you dont have
your phone

they never found it or if they did they
didnt give it to me

its not at the hospital

theres a hospital phone by your bed but
i dont know the number

and u probably cant speak

but i wanted to tell u that im coming in
a week to see u

about what happened it was no
accident lenny p said so and so did
mccarthy

galveston they say its heron galveston
had you run off the road

did you ever talk to him? mccarthy says
heron does his fathers dirty work to
keep his allowance his condo in the city

the guys are going to do something
about it i dont know what

i havent been to the fen except for five
minutes

my mother is in hospital again she said
your name

i too say your name

i say Jack i say kamav tu to your
voicemail

even though maybe your phone is in
the mud under your truck

or the truck has been towed and kept
as evidence or crushed at the dump

and your phone the thread between us
crushed too

Did I press Send? No. I don't think so. But I'm never sure
these days of what I have or have not done.

Trespass

The orchids need watering. That is one thing I can do. Through the heavy shadow at the side of Galveston's place, I make my way to the greenhouse. It isn't locked. The leaves are gasping with nobody to turn on the AC at night. Orchids need cold nights to thrive. Without the AC the orchids will not flower.

I'm trespassing now in the greenhouse. But the orchids — who else will take care of them? I move down the rows of wilted leaves and hungry roots reaching through the meshes. I pick up the fallen petals and tuck them into my palm.

After watering the orchids, I do something even more forbidden. I try the back door of the house. It too is unlocked. The kitchen, where I'd so often had tea with Iris, opens into a hallway with mahogany floors, wood-paneled walls. I feel like a thief, sneaking in here, but now I'm driven to see how these people live, and find myself on stairs wide as our driveway. It's too late to turn back.

A carpeted hall. A banister polished to a quiet glow nobody sees. Upstairs, another hall, a bedroom silent and airless as a shadow. A bed sits on a raised platform like a boxing ring or stage or altar. I imagine dead Louise Galveston lying or thrown across this bed. The wallpaper reveals a repeated landscape: a forest, a deer among trees. A river, bulrushes, water lilies, a dragonfly. This lush false terrain contains no tailings, no poisoned river. The real world is too ugly for this room. Where are the mine shafts, crane lifts, the stackers and crushers?

There is no human touch or disarray. No dust. No sweater or bathrobe thrown over a chair. It's like the setting for a sacrifice or wax museum, and I think of Iris having to be responsible for this chamber of horrors. She told me she'd been instructed to change the sheets twice a week, whether they'd been slept in or not.

There's a noise downstairs. Footsteps in the hall. A man's voice. "Hello? Who's there?"

I don't know how, but I manage to get out unseen.

Primrose and Queenie

Primrose Kowalski comes to my house to clean the kitchen. She comes three days a week. Jack and her father were friends. *Brothers,* she says. *Like this.* She holds up two fingers tight to each other. Her fingers are red. Burned in the fire or raw from cleaning, I don't know which. Probably both. "You may not need the help," she says, "but it's more about the company. My Dad would want me to do something. Anything."

As she cleans, she talks about her sister Coral: how they used to catch frogs as kids, steal tulip leaves from Dalia Doroshenko's garden to make funeral boats for dead dragonflies. How she could still hear Coral's voice calling *Dad, Dad,* then sliding away, melting, swallowed by the smoke from the fire. How the medics covered her body with a sheet so that Primrose wouldn't see.

I don't tell her that Coral sang her lament and spoke to me as I stood at the river.

Primrose does my laundry, laughing as the sheets billow and lift on the clothesline. She brings them in and we fold them, Primrose at one end and me at the other.

"Why do you laugh so much?" I ask.

"I kind of have to," she says with a shrug.

Primrose is engaged to Cyril Lepke. Cyril with his mullet and Primrose with her long brown braid. She's like the golden air of late summer heat, afternoon light. Not the yellow of bruises or decay, but of sunshine. That's what she brings into the house, and I am grateful to have her here.

Today, Primrose brings Queenie with her. That first sighting comes back to me: Queenie, silver, polished, eel-like, flitting down the aisles of Food World. Standing at the door, smiling too widely and watching me with veiled bright eyes, Queenie could be a creature from a folk tale, the kind that quietly slips its spores under your skin. A tale not for children.

"Queenie saved me after the fire," says Primrose. "She healed my burns." Primrose raises her sleeve, lifts her blouse, turns to show me the welts on her arm, the map of scars across her back, the reddened scape of her stomach. "You should have seen them before. What a mess. But Queenie, like I said, she saved me. She was my sister's closest friend."

"That's right," says Queenie, fluttering her fingers in the direction of Nurses Creek. A lick of fear like foxfire slides across the back of my neck. "Some day, sooner or later, Coral and I will be reunited," she says.

Dream 3

In the fen, my toes slide against the dissolving knotted stems of water lily, pickerel weed.

I step on something that moves. It's too big for plant or animal. This moving thing, almost dead or dying in the water. The water is brown around it as the thing sheds matter and new life. Pulsing flicks, embryonic. Now the water clears. I expect to see a fallen log, melting in this marshy soup. But it's Jack who lies below me. My shrouded Jack, I try to lift him from the water. Where is the tube for his throat? A water lily stem can bring the air into his lungs. But the water lily stems are too slippery and Jack's too heavy. I can't lift him. I can't step over him. I can't go back. Jack is not in my bed to wake me from my screaming.

Pie 3

After the sun has gone down and I'm alone, the stranger knocks again at my door. I see him clearly this time: an organized face, symmetrical, that slender sharp nose, eyes the deep blue of night sky. He's holding a meat pie, his signet ring glinting in the dim light of the hall.

And I recognize him. He's the man of the park, of the coral-colored rose, the secret I'd almost forgotten.

"The pie, it's nothing special," he says. "Just from the bakery."

Without being invited, again he takes off his shoes and leaves them at the door. His hands are clean. Even so, he washes them at the sink. He heats the meat pie in the microwave and gets out two plates and knives and forks. He moves quietly on his long legs, like a man possessing the earth he walks on. Already, I'm seeing myself from above, my body folded. Faced with this man, I have no right or strength, and feel my will, my thoughts leaking away. We sit across from each other at the kitchen table. He puts his cellphone beside his plate. "In case there's a call I need to take," he says. "An emergency. You never know."

Could such a quiet, commanding man have an emergency? He's in charge of my kitchen and the world; if an emergency arose, he'd put his finger on it and the crisis would dissolve.

I look at the pie on my plate. "I'm not hungry," I say.

"Eat," says the stranger. "I can tell you're not eating. Is nobody taking care of you?"

My reply is not an answer to his question. "Jack," I say. I push away my plate. Jack in the hospital bed, Jack in his shroud of skin. He'd welcome this caring stranger. I see him sitting across from this man and me, piling our plates with food, pouring tea, later whiskey. *Jack. Everything in me misses everything in you. Everything in me needs you.*

"Who's Jack?"

"My husband."

The stranger spears a morsel of the pie with his fork and holds it out before me. "Jack would want you to eat." The stranger's nails are filed and the cuticles neatly trimmed. With his polished hand he feeds me. Another piece. "That's better," he says. I sit back, subdued, slack, limp.

Later he makes tea. I look at the cup in front of me.

"Is it too hot?" asks the stranger. He picks up the spoon. "I'll stir it for you, to cool it down."

Suddenly I can't think about eating or drinking, when my Jack cannot move, must be turned from side to side, can only breathe with a tube in his throat. I push my chair from the table.

"Are you all right?" the stranger asks, leaning toward me. I'm crying. He moves his chair to sit beside me. I cry against his white shirt. If I don't look at him I can believe he's not here, but his rich man's perfume is in the air and filling my lungs.

Sometime later, I wake up in bed, the sheet below me soaked. The air around me thick with neglect. With the smell of bandages needing changing. The stranger's body beside me is naked, stretched out over our marriage bed. He's snoring.

I can't stay here in this bed. *Get up, move, move,* and I stumble into the living room. The place in my body once filled by Jack, by the vivid green light of the fen, by my mother's stories and her spiky, difficult love, where has that place gone? I can't feel it, can't find it. I rampage through the house, pulling sheets and towels from the closets, dishes from the cupboards. I can't find it. I can't remember what I'm looking for.

Sometime before dawn I go back to the bedroom. The bed is empty. I can't lie down on these damp crushed sheets, on the depression made by my body and the body of the stranger. The floor tilts under me. I can't stay here.

When I run to the front door, I expect to see the world cap-sized. The remains of houses and chewed-up streets, pickup trucks overturned like beetles. Torn-up lawns, twisted roof joists, drywall fragments, folded shells of aluminum siding, slabs of asphalt in the road. But everything's the same.

Disgust can be so ordinary. The driveway rises from the road to the house, the tree in our yard spreads its branches, the vault of the sky still soars over the town, and the morning sun burns off the dew.

Then Rose is here, getting out of her truck, walking up the driveway with a stack of frybread wrapped in a tea towel.

"Are you okay?" she says. She stops short, as if a barrier has dropped between us. I tell her yes, of course I'm okay. Rose shouldn't be here. Nobody should be here. This house is defiled.

"I can come in?" she asks, looking at me too closely. I pull myself back. I don't want her inside my house, inside its mess. I lie. "The shower's running." She reaches and I let her hug me. She hands me the frybread and I'm already in the door before her truck backs down the drive.

The Next Thing

What do you do? The next thing. The next thing is the only thing you can do.

Rose's frybread is still warm. Rescue bread. I hold it against my face. I think of her hands shaping the dough. The fat spattering in the pan. I put the frybread on the kitchen table. For a moment, the floor's steady under my feet.

In the shower, I scrub my skin raw. I take the sheets off the bed and take them to the garage. I pour bleach on the mattress. I fill the pail with water and more bleach, and scour the walls and windows and the bedroom floor, then the bed frame, the night tables, the dresser. I empty the drawers. I throw my clothes into the washing machine, set the dial to heavy duty, long wash, extra rinse. I run the washing machine twice.

The teacups, the teapot, plates, forks are still on the kitchen table where I'd sat with him. The fork is on my plate. There are a few crumbs. Half the meat pie remains. It's in its pie plate beside my tea cup, the spoon still on the saucer. The teapot half full. I take it all outside to the garbage can.

Irene Slepchik is sweeping her sidewalk. She stops her sweeping in mid stroke, looks at me hard. She says, "Are you okay there, girl?"

I hear myself say *why wouldn't I be?*

Irene frowns. "But you aren't," she says. "Are you?" She starts sweeping again, slowly. She watches me while she sweeps. "Throwing all them dishes out. Perfectly good dishes."

I go inside and run another shower. I can never get clean enough. When I come out of the bathroom, Irene is at the front door. She's holding a plate of perogies.

"Eat," she says. She sits down at the table to watch me, her mouth a straight line. I stare at the plate. I don't have time for perogies. I need to clean. That is the next thing. Purity against the defiled. I need to clean every surface in the kitchen. Everywhere he stepped. Everything he touched. Every bit of this house that watched what happened. Then I'll clean the bathroom, and have another shower.

Am I eating? Yes, I am. Now I can't stop. The perogies melt on my tongue.

"Keep going," Irene says, nodding. I eat faster and faster. I reach for Rose's frybread. I eat three pieces. I hear my mother. *Don't stuff yourself like that.* What kind of hunger is this? I eat three more. It isn't hunger. I can stop whenever I want. I don't want. I'm defiled by this need.

"Where's the fire?" says Irene with a nervous laugh. She turns away from me as if she can't bear to witness this, but keeps watch from the corner of her eye. "Slow down." She takes the frybread from my hand. "Later," she says. "Eat later."

Dread

You climb down from the train in Toronto and claw through the crowds at Union Station. You want to see Jack. You don't want to see him. You're scared. No, not scared — you're filled with body-crawling dread. In the hospital there are red and pink chrysanthemums at the nursing station. Two nurses sitting on chairs. One on the phone and one at a computer. "No," says the one on the phone. "That isn't right."

The nurse knows. Maybe she is not a nurse. Maybe a judge. How straight and strict she is. *That isn't right.* Why is a judge sitting in the nursing station? You turn your head away and hurry past, in case she sees you. As you rush down the impossibly long hall, a green curtain is pulled around a bed. The hooks of the curtain swish along the metal track, and a bright voice speaks on the other side of the curtain. This has nothing to do with you.

Dread. Such dread to see your husband. You count the steps to his door. The closer you get, the higher the dread slides up your spine. A thin, icy geyser. As you approach, a smiling nurse emerges from the room. "He's out of his coma," she says.

His coma? As if a coma belongs to him, is a part of his body or a garment he can step into and out of. Could you, too, step into and out of your betrayal of your beautiful Jack?

That isn't right isn't right.

You stand at the door, your transparent face reflected in the narrow window, and beyond it the real, embodied shape on the bed.

You sit in the sagging chair beside the bed and the night before last is beside you. Jack's eyes are open. He looks as if he's smiling. He lifts his hands and when you lean in, his bandaged arms are around you. You're shaking, your weight's against him. Even though he tries to hang on, his arms are weak. With a strange unfamiliar mouth he tries to whisper into your ear. You think you hear your name, but you're not sure. When you get up to leave you turn away from your reflection in the window.

You have lifted yourself so lightly out of this life.

In the bathroom of Irene Slepchik's niece's apartment, you wash your face. You look in the mirror. You see the ordinary face of Orchid looking back. A downturned face, hollow and unforgiving. You see this face as a fly does. Through many thousand different lenses.

Rehab

The edges of clouds are sutured over the bright sky, and a small blue fragment remains. The blue feels false. Without this refracted light, the sky would be as black as the deepest, siltiest part of the orchid fen.

I'm going, again, to save Galveston's orchids in spite of him. The greenhouse orchids can't support themselves. They're trapped; they'll never see the sky, blue or black. They'll never feel a rummaging bee. They have to be pollinated by hand. Everything about them must be mediated by a human hand, or they die.

Like Jack, saved by the grace of a human hand. Or maybe by something else. *We've got Jack covered*, said Coral Kowalski. The still green waters are deep, the bodies of dead girls dissolving into all of it.

They're moving Jack to rehab, somewhere in Toronto. Do the tributaries, the underground rivers run that far?

I too would like to be saved by a human hand. And if not that, by an undoing of time. Outside the greenhouse window, competing winds have pushed the clouds together and the last false blue of the sky has disappeared. The clouds are like the teeth of a zipper fastened over a wound.

Picnic

We bring my mother home from the hospital in Primrose Kowalski's truck. Women have gathered on the porch, and Mam cries when she sees them: Irene Slepchik, Queenie, Rose, and Iris Blythe, whom I haven't seen since we were fired. I don't know why Mam's crying. Her knees buckle, but we catch her.

"Thank you," she says to the women. "Thank you." Her face is soft for them. Clinging to Primrose and me, she inches forward, her feet not lifting from the ground.

"Careful up the steps," says Primrose, "nice and slow."

Iris barges ahead. "Look," she says, turning back to us as she rummages through a shopping bag. "I brought us a picnic. Salmon sandwiches and a cake." I don't want to see her or eat her food, but I'm unsure how to get rid of her. She follows us down to the birch grove.

The leaves here are still gold but paler now, thinner, admitting more scattered light through the branches. It's as though we were meant to see them this way. On the bus to Toronto, on the driver's small portable radio, a scientist was saying that without our gaze, nothing — including this birch grove — would have any color. What we see are light waves of differing lengths refracting off each surface.

When Jack's alone at night in his room at the rehab hospital, does he have a color? When he shuts his eyes in pain are they grey-green or a hue of nothing? The scientist said that everything outside the human gaze ranges from white to black, so that unobserved places and unobserved lives have no color. In Carminetown, there's so much that's hidden, so many lives uncounted, unseen, so much darkness in the cavern of this place. The panni raklies and their vengeance against the unseen things that have happened here, the panni raklies awash in the lime-green waters of Nurses Creek — they're necessary. They've always been necessary. They make us see the deep hidden truths of our lives. Of the world we're in.

Iris is passing out her salmon sandwiches. I can't look at her, I want her gone. The splinter of her easy sharp bigotry is still stuck under my skin. She says she's happy because she gets to watch her reality TV all day every day now that she doesn't work for the Galvestons. Nothing interferes with her fantasy, not even us. Before I know what's happening, she's laughing, feigning shock and delight, pushing the splinter deeper: them Gypsies, their dresses, their loud voices, their stolen money.

Not this. Especially not in front of my mother, who's half out of her chair now, and wheezing, "Who the hell do you think you are?" Iris doesn't hear my mother over her own laughter.

"Iris," I say. "I don't want to hear about your show. Nobody wants to hear about it."

"How can you not see it?" Iris is pleading. "They don't do nothing, just scam and steal and sit around with their welfare checks, and what about us hardworking people, all that money comes out of our pockets."

She stops cold. She must be seeing something in me that she's never noticed before, or that she's never stopped to notice.

"Iris!" If I'm shouting, I don't care. "I'm one of those people they make fun of in that show of yours." My secret has exploded to the surface. I no longer see the leaves or the stream or the hundred shades of green drifting in from the forest. I see the sandwich in her hand as it falls apart, a mess of salmon and mayonnaise dripping onto her shoe. She keeps her eyes to the ground. Rose watches us, but says nothing. I think of my mother's shame, of mine. Shame with its different complexions. Different depths.

Iris changes color. She's grey now. When she turns to me, to my mother and her dark look, she crumples like waxed paper and turns her face toward me; I know she wants me to see her tears, to see that I've wounded her, and in the face of her tears, I'm meant to apologize, soothe and soften, offer comfort.

Iris picks up her shopping bag. She turns her back to us and slips around the side of the house.

Now color returns to the birch grove. No one speaks about my secret, exposed and still bubbling at the surface, and we stay under the trees till the sun lowers itself over the forest. The color fades quickly. The moment the air cools, we gather around my mother and walk her up through the gardens and inside.

Seeing

After the half-disaster of the backyard picnic, Rose and I see more of each other. It's not deliberate, like making plans for coffee or shopping. It's more like a recognition, an acknowledgement of who we are in our deepest places. But unspoken. Something in me wants to, has to, be with something in her, and we gravitate to each other, talking on the phone, texting; we eat together, drink tea, walk.

Today, in the garden under the sun, Rose turns to my exposed secret. "What was that thing with Iris Blythe?"

"What thing?"

"At that picnic, when we brought your mother home from the hospital. Something went on between you two, and she disappeared."

"I can't remember."

"Come off it, Orchid." She says this kindly, as an aunt or older sister might. "You remember."

She's right. I try to slide away from this, saying something about how Mam had just gotten out of the hospital, how I was still so worried about Jack, but Rose presses on.

"You and your mother," she says, "it's like you're always look-ing over your shoulders." My hands go to my stomach to hide what Rose has already seen. "Always waiting for the ax to drop," she says.

Now my mother's voice is in my ear, close and loud. She reminds me of how we need to watch out; how we have to read people, sharply, and with care, calculate in a split second what they might do or say, and them thinking we're magic because of this. That we have the sight. That it's dukkering, knowing what might happen, telling us when to run, where to hide. But it's not dukkering when the thing most feared happens again and again, in every town, for all of our history.

Mam's list is in front of my eyes: those hundreds of years of being chased, hunted for sport, torn by dogs, enslaved, branded. That's right, Mam said, dozens of times from my earliest childhood memory, her face close to mine. Branded. With a V for Vagabond. Yes, that's what they did way back when. Or the mushes, they had their ears cut off. Then she'd remind me about her father's grandfather back in England. They caught him. He was hanged without trial because they said he stole a horse.

With my eyes closed against my mother and her stories, I try to pull myself from the mud I'm in, only to step into future muck. I hear her voice. *Don't ever forget.* In my mind, I'm running, keeping pace, talking so quickly I don't know how to stop. Words around words around words, like mud churning the water.

"Orchid?" Rose is crying. I'm crying. She touches my arm.

I'm here. Still in the back yard, still sitting in the hard aluminum chair. Not running, not hunted. But my fingers are clenched around my arms.

I have to get out of here. Go somewhere, anywhere.

When I stand, Rose slips her arm around me and we go up the road and through the town, past my mother's empty house. Without knowing or caring why, we laugh.

Dalia Doroshenko, surrounded by a cloud of dust, is sweeping her driveway. We stand on the sidewalk in front of her and laugh. Our laughter takes our breath and bends us double till we're crying again. Dalia does not speak. This woman who once cared for me like a mother turns her back and goes inside. There are many women like Dalia Doroshenko in this town, Rose says, and if they knew who Orchid Lovell really is, they'd turn their backs on me too. Clerks would follow me around stores, hoping to catch me stealing a can of tuna or a hairbrush, fake nails, potato chips, a package of single-slice cheese, anything. This makes me laugh again. Rose's laughter tells me she understands why my mother needed us to be invisible. My laughter reaches out to Rose.

When you look at me, don't draw a line between before the telling and after. I am the same person.

The street before me turns sharp and bright like a dream. Rose quiets. She says, "Orchid, I have to tell you something." There's no laughter in her voice now. "I'm going away," she says. "In September." She has been accepted at a university, where she will study something I forget because her words hit me like a tree falling.

Wildcat

My mother is drawing the moon again, and I watch her hand move across the page in smooth strokes. "Each time I look at the moon now, I think of Jack," she says. She puts down the binoculars. "Is it possible he knew something about me that I didn't know myself?" She lifts the paper to show me her moon drawing: the crisp light and deep pitted shadows. Jack, too, down in rehab, wrapped in fluorescent light and deep shadow.

"Mam, you have a real talent."

"Yes." She looks pleased. "One I didn't know I had." She lifts the binoculars again, and resumes drawing. "I'm on the road to thinking he might be okay for you, that mush," she says. She tells me he's learning. The food, the cleaning. The pure kept inside, dirt outside. Before she asks me to leave, she says, "You need to visit him. I can tell you've been without him too long." Her words are surprising, but they land in a deep hollow inside me. Jack seems too far away. I'm used to not having him around anymore.

"I'll be fine!" she says. "Go to him. Don't worry about me."

In the morning I take the train. The rehab hospital is in a Toronto suburb, a series of buildings set among wide lawns mowed short. Here, my crime is diminished, a thin curtain pulled across a window. Inside, Jack's looking out over the lawns, a new cellphone on his table.

"Hey, you," he says, smiling as if he's just learned how. He shows me a text from Mac McCarthy. The miners are planning a wildcat strike. Jack tells me this could go either way — the miners could force the bosses to meet their demands or it could result in a crackdown — but he's worried. The Galvestons are brutes. They're thugs. Jack knows this intimately.

"Something's gonna happen," he says. "I can feel it."

Now he's sounding like the panni raklies. I want to ask him if he's getting their telepathic cellphone alerts, but he doesn't need jokes right now.

"Something's gonna happen," he says again. "The town has to look after itself. And you. You gotta look after yourself."

I'm with Jack for hours before I get up to leave. It's still difficult to see his eyes through the layers of swollen skin now faded to yellow. The yellow of my nighttime nausea. When I turn my back, the color will be gone, there will be no yellow, and the sickening moment might disappear, dissolve into the non-color of my unconscious.

But this absence still holds the stranger's smell. I'll have to buy a new bed.

The aching distance between us will disappear when Jack comes home. When we're together again in the new bed, Jack and Orchid will be Jack and Orchid as we always were.

You want to go back to that place of Jack and Orchid. You'll go back to the fen and the perfumed fen love, the damselfly love, the orchid love. You'll look into each other's eyes and know a repair has been made. Just a small one.

Black Van

The air roars with voices as the miners walk back and forth outside the locked mine gates. I can't make out what they're shouting. The crowd around them is agitated, jittery, as if waiting for something to happen. Off to the side, Carminetown's few activists and many wives are doling out sandwiches and coffee. Primrose Kowalski is here, surrounded by a knot of women. Then, as she climbs onto a wooden box, the energy of the crowd shifts. The people go silent.

"My dad Gord," she calls out to the crowd. "My sister Coral. They killed them. But Jack Bachinski —" Someone hands her a bullhorn and she brings it to her lips. "They tried with Jack and they failed. They failed. Now it's our time." Her voice tears through the gates to the thin glass windows of the office block where shadowed figures have gathered, watching.

Primrose turns toward each face in the crowd. "We're working people trying to live our best lives. Care for our families. Are they going to kill us one by one?"

As if in answer to this question, a van turns onto the street, black like a shadow carved out of the day. It revs its engine, picking up speed, bearing down on the crowd. Some people try to stand their ground, some scatter and run. Screams, shouts.

Get away, run.

Irene Slepchik throws herself at the van, her fake red nails flashing. "May your children shit in your soup!" she hollers before two men pull her back.

The van goes for Primrose, and with a heavy thud, sends her body into the air. She drops from a great height, and before she hits the ground, I'm running, slipping on loose gravel in my effort to reach her, but somebody pulls me back, drags me to the edge of the road. It's Mac McCarthy. His face is red and furious. "Go! Go home, Orchid! Hasn't Jack already been through enough?"

Swearing at Mac, tearing myself away, I'm falling back, landing hard on the gravel. Small stones in my palms, in my knees when I pull myself up. My hands are sticky with blood but I'm up and running again. The miners, my neighbors, my friends have gathered around Primrose.

McCarthy shouts again, and his voice is drowned by the sound of sirens. An ambulance is already speeding toward the mass of shouting people. "You're not safe here, Orchid." McCarthy's still yelling somewhere behind me. "Go home!"

I came here for Jack, to be his eyes, his mouth, his voice, to call him on his new cellphone and tell him that Primrose Kowalski spoke his name. But I won't tell him that Galveston's black van hit her, that her body flew into the air, and fell. No. I won't tell him any of this.

Down the road, away from the gates, a car is parked on the shoulder. Some low, sleek thing. A few of the miners have broken away from the crowd at the gates and are running toward the car. One of them has a shovel, another a crowbar. "He's here!" they're yelling. But the car drives through the men, tears around the corner, and is gone.

Clean Hands

Critical condition, life-threatening. That's what the reporter is saying. In the wake of this news, Carminetown descends into a silence so dark it changes the shapes of streets, buildings, yards. The town is flattened. Nothing looks like itself: not the sky, the grass, the gravel at the side of the road. Not the peeling paint of the houses, the untended gardens, the laundry dripping from the clotheslines. Children's bikes are scattered across the lawns. I'm numb with the news about Primrose, but I need to do something. Anything. There are endless possibilities within this anything. I dwell in this space of possibility all day, until a rust-streaked sunset reminds me of Irene Slepchik's red claws.

What vengeance could I carry out with her claws?

This question catches me off guard. Am I really the kind of person to expand into such a violent possibility? Yes, I am. For Primrose I am. If Primrose dies, her whole family will have been wiped out. No vengeance could equal the horror of this loss.

Night comes early. It takes over. No night has felt blacker. A rage inside the women of Carminetown has been freed up in the dark, and they surge through the streets around the Sylvanite Hotel.

"Say her name," a woman calls. "Say her name."

A small knot of weeping men appears, and they answer as one. "Primrose Kowalski," they call back to the women. "Primrose Kowalski, Coral Kowalski, their dad Gord."

As if in a single body, the women turn and move through the town to Galveston's house, and by this time they're screaming. "Say her name," over and over, "Say her name." Somebody throws a stone, and a window breaks.

Their names are on my tongue, all the lost women of the river.

In the morning, the same reporter stands in front of a quilt that has been hung on the mine gates. The women of the town and the reserve have sewn and beaded across its surface the names of the lost women. "So, how long have you been working on this quilt?" he asks.

The women look at each other. "Forever," one of them says.

The reporter looks puzzled. "What has this got to do with the mine?"

"Everything here has to do with the mine."

"And what inspired you?"

Another says, "Look at the names." The reporter tries a different question, and all the woman says is, "Look at the names."

Exhausted, numb, I turn off the TV, and still hear the woman's voice.

Look at the names.

There will be too many names. But here's Primrose on the front page of the newspaper, alive, alive, looking up at me from a hospital bed. She nearly didn't make it, says the article. But she's strong, and has already lost more than a person should lose. The driver of the van, a man not from here, is charged with careless driving. Even though he gets bail, he breaks down and tells the reporter about his three children. Below the picture of Primrose is a courtroom sketch of this man crying. The Galvestons aren't mentioned. Not once.

Sickened, not surprised, I turn the page, and here, across the entire middle section, is a picture of my night visitor. The quiet stranger who fed me, who poured the tea, washed the cups. The devil-man of my bed, handing an oversized check to the mayor. They're both smiling. *Heron Galveston Launches First Annual Louise Galveston Smart City Award with Check to Carminetown for $50,000.* The money is for a women's shelter. His hands are clean. The immaculate hands of Heron Galveston, fragrant, silky, well-scrubbed, like he washes the blood off them a thousand times a day.

Bed 1

At the orchid fen I give thanks. There are no secrets here anymore. Heron Galveston doesn't know me. A man like him, a man who wears his power like an extra skin, he knows my name, yes, but he doesn't know what's hidden behind the name, under *my* skin. I kneel in the place where I first met Jack, where he found me with my hands around the orchid. Where he said, *Wanna be known as the orchid-killer?* The almost-stolen orchid still grows here. The petals have fallen, but the frail stem still stands straight, and the edges of the remaining leaves are worn, as if trampled or bitten. That's me.

The sun has reached its apex, but as I move through the fen, it slides behind the trees. Instead of going home, I veer to the other side of town, and end up at Nurses Creek. The panni raklies are out.

There's a new girl. A slasher. I recognize the raised skin on her arms and stomach like stitches that hold together her dissolving body. Did she do this to herself before she was killed? After? All possibilities are a thinly sliced horror. The other panni raklies put their arms around her, comb her hair, place a grassy wreath on her head. If she wasn't already dead, I'd say she's dying of despair. Even with the crown of reeds, her hair hangs over her downturned face. Her languid fingers trail in the water. How terrible that such things follow you even after leaving this world. Heron Galveston would want to have saved this girl for his women's shelter. Fly her like a flag. She'd be guaranteed to bring praise and pity and donations.

Where is the shelter for the rest of the wounded women? For the fen? The land?

Coral's holding a cellphone, showing it to the girls. "They nearly got Primrose," she says. The panni raklies gather around her as she reads what happened to her sister. She drops the cellphone into the water.

I go home to my bed. No longer the bed of Jack and Orchid. The devil-man is lord of this bed.

Bed 2

I drag the old bed to the front porch and order one from a liquidation sale.

"Why," says Mam, pushing out onto the porch before I can stop her. "Why are you getting rid of a perfectly good bed?"

"It sags."

"How can a new bed sag?"

"It just does."

She's looking at the bed and then at me. There's a nervous energy in her body that says *something's going on.*

"Mother, nothing's going on. It's just not a good bed."

On the day of the new bed's delivery the whole street gathers.

"Go away," I yell, waving as if I could send them all home. "It's only a bed. The fen's going to be torn up, Galveston's sending out his thugs, they nearly killed Primrose, and all you people can do is gawk at my bed."

The movers hoist it onto their shoulders, and kids on their bikes ride circles around them. "Get the fuck outta here," the men say. They carry the bed up the steps into the house. My neighbors are whispering about the quality and thickness of the mattress. About the height of the box spring. About the price.

"Why are you getting a new bed?" yells Mrs. Doherty from two houses down.

"It's for Jack," I shout. "It's orthopedic."

"That ain't orthopedic," says Mrs. Doherty. She goes back inside, slamming the door behind her.

Irene Slepchik comes over to me on the sidewalk. She's wearing her red glue-on combat nails. "Orchid," she whispers in my ear. "The devil was in that old bed." She nods her head. "It's cursed," she says. She points her red claw at me. "You're right to get rid of it."

Darlin

On my way to visit Primrose in the hospital, I buy new sheets. They're blue, the color of 2 a.m. I'll burn the old ones in the incinerator and Mam will shout out the window to ask why. Primrose's hospital sheets are blue too, light as daybreak. Rose is beside her, braiding her cousin's hair. Wrapped in bandages tight around her body, Primrose moves stiffly as she tries to sit up. A cup of water sits on her tray beside a dish of half-eaten applesauce. I lift the cup to Primrose's lips and she drinks. After a minute she gestures with her one good hand that she's had enough.

"Them bastards," she says, breathing heavily. "This is for you, Heron Galveston." I don't know what she means at first, but slowly and with great effort Primrose raises her middle finger. Rose and I laugh, a little nervously.

"Last night I dreamed about Coral. My Coral." She pauses, looks toward the window. "Funny," she says, "this is the first time I've dreamed about her since the fire."

She looks up and smiles at a giant bouquet of gladiolas coming through the door. Behind the bouquet is Cyril Lepke. His mullet is gone, and somehow he's bigger than his body, no longer weedy.

"There's my darlin," Cyril says in a voice quiet and deep as a pond. After he settles into a chair beside the bed, he turns to Rose and me, tells us he's the new shop steward. They're negotiating a contract. "But nothing's ever over," says Cyril. "And that new mine. Shit. Who knows what the new mine will bring."

Burning the Sheets

Jack's incinerator is an old oil drum he keeps at the back of the garden, like everybody does in Carminetown. I drop the devil sheets into the drum, douse them with fire starter. After the initial catch, they smoke for a long time until a small flame grows and keeps growing. The burning sheets erupt in orange flames and black smoke. They smell of fire starter and fire retardant. They still smell of Heron Galveston. Mam yells from her window to know what the hell am I burning, and I say, "Garbage."

All the Shit

At the hospital, Cyril had said he'd build Jack a ramp, but today the orderlies bring the wheelchair up the steps. Then they carry Jack, seated on their linked arms. His weakened body is light. They bring him to the bed and lay him across the deep blue sheets.

"Orchid," says Jack, lifting his hand to mine. "My Orchid of the fen. I'm home. I'm really home." He closes his eyes. I watch him as he sleeps, but I don't entirely recognize him. Not because of how he looks, but because of the way we were pulled apart. He's in a world I can't enter. We're two separate beings on either side of a life we once lived together.

When he wakes, I bring soup made with the last of the cabbages from the garden. "Just to warn you," I tell him as I set the steaming bowl on his tray, laughing to hide my self-consciousness, "it's probably terrible."

"Not bad," says Jack after swallowing the first spoonful. "You've been practicing while I was away." He tries for a laugh, but it turns into a groan. "My ribs," he says, laughing anyway. His hand shakes as it lifts the spoon. Soup dribbles down his chin.

Later, in bed, he reaches for me. We lie together, joined and separate. I want and don't want to touch him. I worry about what my touch will tell him, what he'll feel. We're different now; we're before and after, a line dividing our lives.

Outside our window, the trees reach into the darkness. Our night-blue sheets are swallowed into this dark. There is no floor, no ceiling, there are no sides. We could be suspended over a body of silent water. The world out there can't speak to us. It has no tongue.

"Being away from you," says Jack, "it was like a betrayal. We were betrayed by all the shit that took me from you." He doesn't know the truth of his words. He doesn't know how devastating this truth has been.

Queenie and the Veil

Primrose, leaning heavily on a cane, makes her way into the kitchen. She shakes her head, refusing to talk about her injuries. She's not alone. "You remember Queenie," she says.

The hospital has sent Queenie to care for Jack. Standing in the kitchen, she emits an uncanny glow. I imagine amorphous wings sprouting from her back, hands ready to pull Jack into a world of dizzying light and shadow. I didn't ask for a caregiver, but here she is, smiling widely and handing me a sheaf of papers with her long, pointed fingers. When she sees me looking, she laughs and recites her qualifications as if they're a joke.

"I'm just an ordinary old PSW," she says, snapping blue nitrile gloves over her hands. "And," in a sly whisper, leaning in too close, "I want the Galvestons dead." Standing at the bedroom door — now the shore of Queenie's world — I watch her as she takes over Jack's care. Her gestures and movements speed up and then turn languorous, hypnotic, as if out of time.

In the garden, out of earshot, I call the hospital. Can they send another PSW? No, there is no other PSW available. Can I send Queenie away anyway? No, this is strongly discouraged, since Mr. Bachinski needs full-time professional home care without which he'll have to recuperate in a nursing home. I will not send Jack to a nursing home.

When I turn to go back inside, Queenie is hanging our new sheets on the clothesline. She tells me that she boiled them on the stove for two hours. How this is possible, I don't know.

"Everything has to be sterile for your husband," she says in a businesslike voice. "We can't take any chances." While the sheets are drying, we play cards and drink tea. Primrose and Queenie offer to make supper.

I will learn to accept Queenie. I have no choice. When she talks about Coral, her eyes well up. Is she summoning the panni raklies? Suddenly I'm terrified at the thought of meeting them outside Nurses Creek — in the street after the Sylvanite has closed, in the dark hall outside our bedroom, dripping and singing to Jack at his bedside.

At least she has none of the signs of the dead: no greenish pallor, no deep-set rot working its way to the surface. Still, with Queenie in our house, the veil between the two worlds rips at the edges, and I struggle to pull myself back into our ordinary, real kitchen with its yellow walls, its scrubbed linoleum floor.

"Hey," says Primrose, laughing. "Where are you? Come back." She's putting a plate of fried eggs and tomatoes and bacon on the table in front of me. Her bright eyes say, *I was almost one of them but here I am.*

Jack's Wrist

On the night after Queenie's arrival, I go to Nurses Creek, call out across the water. I ask the panni raklies to tell me what to do. They float over from the other shore, watch me with their sunken eyes, but say nothing. If their silence is also a prophecy, I don't know what to make of it.

I walk home to a dark house. My mother's asleep, Jack's asleep. The walls close in. I am now looking after two people who are shuffling back into life. It is too much.

In the morning, I don't remember if I slept. I watch Jack in bed. His right foot has been uncovered in the night and a thin hair-like root pushes out between his toes. A tendril curls from his ear. The rise in my stomach tells me this is Queenie's doing.

At breakfast I ask her: "Did the river spirits send you?" On the surface this sounds like a stupid question.

Queenie must think so too. "A long time ago — and what's time, anyway? — I went through a dark door and came back," she says. "Now this is how I am. This is what happens." She smiles her dazzling smile.

Later we bathe Jack in warm water steeped with bruised plantains. We run the cloth down his back, and I find the old shape of his body under the flaking yellow skin. I look for the root and the tendril, but they don't show themselves. Maybe they're the aftermath of a dream.

Jack's hand reaches toward Queenie, and her fingers, long as stems, caress his arm. They close around his wrist, her fingertips stroking his deep blue veins. She seems to fade in and out, like she's still passing through that dark door, and pulling him with her. This movement, this intimacy, is unbearable.

"Queenie, please stop."

"This is what I do," she says. Her eyes are clear as a child's. "I restore life. It's my job. That's all. He'll come back to you, I promise." The smile stretches across her face. For a brief second there's a smile inside the smile.

The Gift

I order quilting fabric online. While waiting for the delivery, which takes days, I find my mother's needles and thread, and set up her sewing machine. When my package arrives, dropped in the middle of the driveway where anybody could steal it, the colors take my breath away. The greens of shallow rivers and reeds, the purplish blues of wild iris and pickerel weed, the deep blue of early night sky, cool white of water lily, warm white of cotton grass. I imagine sewing a design of entwined fen plants: stems, leaves and flowers. But I don't have the skill. Instead, I make a simple pattern for a table runner for Rose. It's not practical, I know. What use does a university student have for a table runner?

When it's finished, I invite Rose to the garden and present it to her. "You could put it on your bed. Or across your desk. Or you could hang it on the wall."

Rose brings the table runner to her face, then unfolds it across both our laps. We sit shoulder to shoulder, the runner across our knees, until we no longer hear the voices of neighborhood children, and the smells of cooking drift through the streets.

Rose, I'll miss you. You are one of the few who understands this life.

I can't say this aloud. My words are sewn into her gift.

Gone

A yog's in the yard, gone now to embers. We're cooking up a good supper in Mam's cast iron pot. Cabbages. Onions. Carrots. Plain, reassuring food. Jack sleeps while we cook, and the sun passes below the branches of the trees. The color has leached from the forest. All day my mother has been quiet, as if something's gathering.

"I'm sorry," she says as she stirs the pot. "I can never be sorry enough."

I know what's coming. She's revisiting little Heron Galveston, and I'm a child again, with the bitter taste rising, again, when I hear his name. How many more times will I hear this story, my mother offering her reasons, her sorrows, not listening to mine?

She's stabbing sausages with a fork. "I know it was a long time ago." The embers pop, and sparks shoot across the grass. "I didn't want to leave you. But you don't know how badly I needed the money."

The crackling fire doesn't cover that long, loud silence of years. How she loved Heron. Her love is in her voice even now. He was nine or ten when she left me to be someone else's mother. How much of JadeMarie Lovell went into loving Heron Galveston? So much that there was hardly any left for me.

You call every day after school while I sit in Dalia's kitchen eating hot dogs and Cheez Whiz. You talk about my shoes getting too tight and how when your job is finished we'll have enough money for a year and you'll get me new patent leather shoes and a pink pencil case. You ask how is school and have I brushed my teeth, and then tell me to put Dalia on the line. I don't tell you about lying in the bed in her spare room staring at the ceiling and trying not to cry because it isn't my bed or my room or my mother. Dalia isn't murri dai with her arms around me and neither is my loneliness.

And then the job ends suddenly and even though my mother is back in our kitchen, she's crying and still not here. After I waited for her for so long. I make my lunch, clean the house, cook our suppers. I'm ten, then eleven, then twelve. She doesn't come back.

That was how the years unfurled, like a carpet down a dark hall.

Read Them

I never liked my old house except when I was in exile next door. It was like living in a cellar, dark veins of mold nestling in the corners, a wet despair behind the walls. Now we are emptying this house of everything it has ever given or withheld from us.

Packing up our good dishes, I feel no sentimentality about them. My mother wants me to find letters in a box somewhere. I empty her cupboards — blankets, sheets, winter clothes — and finally, at the back of a shelf in her bedroom closet, I find the box.

"Give it here," she says. "Read them."

I don't want to, but she says again, "Read them," already heading toward her room. Before I even open the box, I hear faint sounds of my mother crying.

Letters Not Sent

Friday May 28

Mister Galveston just so you know I didn't steal that little Royal Doulton shepherdess thing, I never stole nothing, it was little Heron broke it and I said Heron you're telling your dad when he comes home and Heron cried. I took him to the kitchen and sat him beside me and gave him a piece of pie and said it's okay Heron and I think he wanted my arms around him more than he wanted the pie. I never knew what he did with the pieces of that Royal Doulton thing b/c he took them I never saw them again. Don't be mad at him. I swear he was scared to tell you.

I did my best for you keeping your house clean and looking after your Heron I left my own child because I needed the job and I could be like an auntie or a mother to yours. There wasn't nothing I wouldn't of done for that little boy after she died. You never saw him crying his eyes out b/c of how you took off after the funeral and he never knew what hit him.

And I think now of what he went through. All alone in the care of me a total stranger and you leaving him at such a time. And making me take him to see her in her coffin like that. The one side of her face covered with flowers so we wouldn't see where it hit the rocks. I can tell you now that it's a real shame.

Yours Truly

JadeMarie Lovell

June 5th

Dear Mister Galveston

You hitting me because of that shepherdess thing Right across the room You'll not forget how I landed against the wall and down on your floor You kicking and yelling at me that it was hers and young Heron crying in the doorway Daddy Daddy stop. I will certainly not forget it.

Yours Truly

JadeMarie Lovell

June 10th

Dear Mister Galveston

Our fowki we get called a lot of things. Mostly it's thieves. It might not be a big deal for

you but for us that word's like a worm burrowing in your skin, rummaging, fattening, filling
up the space where your heart should be, filling
up your whole self till you don't know if you are
the worm or the person.

How much hate comes from that word
simmering in your body like an ancient soup on
the fire. The soup filling you every day. The hate
soup. Even though the truth can thin it out,
pour it off, truth no longer matters because you
believe yourself finally to be what they have
called you A thief of anything figurines bikes
bread oranges hub caps children gardens trees
rivers air etc. etc. etc. You're the thief Mister
Galveston what you did to the land & the water
Plus you only paid me for the first two months
and after that you never paid me nothing I
know I'll never see it though you promised it me
again and again.

At least I have the orchid fen I can go there
and I'm a real person not a thief.

Yours Truly

JadeMarie Lovell

Shame

Where in a woman's body does shame the squatter reside?

Earthquake

When my mother returns to her half-empty kitchen and sits with an exhausted sigh, I stand beside her for the longest time, unable to speak. Then I'm ten years old again, a child watching her mother go out the door with a suitcase, saying, *You'll be just fine with Dalia,* and *I'll call you.* Walking down the road and not looking back.

I want to tell her about Heron Galveston. Not about the boy she knew and loved, but the Heron Galveston of my bed, Heron Galveston of the fire, Heron of the black van that drove through a crowd and lifted Primrose Kowalski's body into the air. Heron Galveston the devil-man, braided into all our lives. Heron's the dark thread from her body to mine, a stitch in my throat that chokes off my voice.

"What's going on?" Mam says.

"Nothing. Really."

I will never be able to uproot Heron Galveston. He's inside me, inside my mother. When we bring the letters home, she won't talk about them. She asks me to burn them in Jack's incinerator. We pack the drum with old newspapers to start the fire, and burn the letters with last week's news.

"I saw Heron the other night," says Mam, "driving along our street in that car of his. I called to him and he remembered me with such a nice smile. He said, *you saved me.* After all those years, he remembered."

She shakes her head. "Poor Heron. Now look at him. All this business about tearing up the fen, his father getting him involved. Heron was such a kind boy. I hardly know what to think."

My mother wants to be alone with the burning letters. I want to be alone with my own burning. Inside, I sweep the floor, wipe the table. Again — forever — I can't get anything clean enough. I pour tea, my hand shaking. The teacup rattles in its saucer. It's like a distant earthquake, only here, in my kitchen. After dark, I go to Nurses Creek. The panni raklies turn their heads to the shore, their damaged eyes looking at me. Through me. I feel them reading every buried thing. They see the knot under my ribs, and woven into this knot all the threads of my life. They reach out to me with their long fingers as if they can undo this tangle.

Just bring him, they say, and I know who they mean.

Walking Through Walls

Queenie you have to go

you don't like me you don't have to like
me i'm not here for you

you want to know if I'm one of your
river spirits, and the answer is no I'm
not dead enough for them I'm not ready
to go and Jack's not ready and they're
not my river spirits

what are you doing with him

Jack's my patient what am I doing? My
best I'm doing my best I won't go till it's
time and it isn't time

I'll lock the door on you
I won't let you in

I can walk through walls

The Dreamer

Under my ribs is the knot. The knot is also a seed. A smallish seed. It's in the way. In the bedroom, I sink into the night-blue sheets, willing the seed to disappear. There's lots of room — Jack still lies at the far edge of the bed in his private cocoon. The ceiling has dissolved in the dark, and I rise through the roof to the stars and the night sky, our bed below them a mirror.

And then I'm at Nurses Creek above the trees, my seed still tight inside me as I gaze down at the tailings, greyish under the half-moon. A blurred shadow steps out of a low-slung car and picks his way in fine leather shoes across the calcified skin of the tailings.

Over here, I say, lowering myself to the river bank.

The smell of that dead water. The ruination. Only a criminal would do this to a river. What if, as a punishment, you had to carry the smell of your crimes in your body? On your breath, your skin, your hair?

Is that you? he calls. *I've wanted to see you again.*

I don't answer. I wait. The seed inside drags through the air in my lungs and it's like being pulled on a string. A string stretched tight. When it breaks, a flame erupts, catches in my chest with the pain of surprise, of connection. The flame that ignited the burning sheets. The blaze that ripped through the house where Coral

Kowalski slept with her family. The flame licks at other fires not extinguished, and grows.

Heron closes in, peeling off his shirt and his trousers. But he is no fen man, wading through the shore grasses with his long pale legs. He drops his keys, his ring, his wallet and his cellphone onto the riverbank, and the seed inside me is crackling, bursting with black flames. They roar up my throat. I'm afraid the trees might catch fire. The flames pour from the burning house, and I am the house.

Heron takes a step back. Most of the panni raklies watch from a distance, but Coral is swimming across the river. It's her time. She has waited for this. They all have. She rolls like a seal, and the water rolls around her. I'm in the river now too — it's viscous and cold like the bodies of the dead girls, and the fire flows over the water. I'm swimming through flames and Heron reaches for me. Hoping I'll save him. He's easy to drag down. His voice from the surface of the water, the surface of the fire, is like a siren's song pulled inside out. *Let me go.* Together, the panni raklies and me, we get him into the river, hold him down. Water snakes bind his ankles, and he flounders, kicks, thrashes for what seems like forever. And then stops.

"What's going on?" says Jack, turning to me.

"Nothing." My body jolts as if I've fallen through the ceiling. "Nothing's going on."

"You were dreaming."

"Yes."

Am I still dreaming? Is that the tendril, longer this time, slipping from his ear? When I look again, there is no tendril. No tendril, no flame. The seed inside me is burned to cinders and replaced by darkness. The dark of Coral's house, charred and soaked with water from the fire hoses, the dark of my house from Dalia's upstairs window. The dark of my mother's absence.

I lift myself from our bed and step out into the night. I try to hold the dark inside me but it keeps spilling out.

At the end of the road across from the tailings, the dark house drips poison onto the land. The charred stain will harden, calcify with the lower strata of this terrain, and in decades or centuries a geologist will study the remains layer by layer and wonder what happened here.

These fragments flow like ribbons ahead of me as I walk across the tailings toward the river. From behind the birches of Nurses Creek I hear the high reedy sound, floating, floating. My only desire in this place is for time to unspool itself, for Jack and me to be dancing again across the tailings to the song shaped by this voice.

The Death

It's Coral Kowalski who's singing, the rise and fall of her voice too beautiful to hear. She's half submerged, greenish and muscular as a salmon, her wreath messy, undone, sliding off her head. She sings to a body floating in the water, face down and rocking gently in the current. A silent water snake, sinking and rising, undulates around this floating shape, and disappears. Heron Galveston's right hand — soft, scrubbed, swollen white skin breaking to reveal the tender pink beneath — is caught on a cedar root jutting into the river.

Baring her teeth, Coral shakes the root, and the hand loosens its grip. Heron Galveston's body, nudged by the current, rolls over, and his envelope of skin, his overburden, slips away. The river coaxes his head from its neck, revealing the upper bones of the spine, remnants of flesh clinging. Lolling in the current, turning to face me, the head tilts gently, opaque eyes open in strange wonder. The water snake surfaces, unhinges her jaws. She fastens them around the head and swims with it to the shallows, where she works it slowly and delicately into her throat. Heron Galveston's jellied innards, ugly as the ruination of the land, unfurl like ribbons. The stink is unimaginable.

His cellphone, wallet, keys, his gold signet ring, his folded clothes are lined up along the shore. And his fine polished shoes.

As I watch, Heron Galveston's body is eaten, dissolved by his corrosive river.

When this process is complete, Coral looks up at me. "Thank you," she says.

Why does she thank me? I was only the dreamer of this death.

The Pivot

On the TV, a reporter standing in front of flashing lights and police cars discusses the drowned body of Heron Galveston, found this morning in Nurses Creek back of the old Galveston Mines dry tailings. Behind the reporter a shrouded shape is loaded into an ambulance. The reporter says shock, tragedy, investigation, police, coroner, inquest, and so on.

What do we do? We do the next thing.

On my phone, a red alert flashes. The message hijacks my screen like a regional emergency notification, but it's from the panni raklies: prophecy doesn't come out of thin air. Using predictive text, their swamp phones foretell the future. All life pivots on this moment.

The Future

Hey, Galveston empire. Now that we've fed your son to your poisonous river, what next? We've decayed here in Nurses Creek for far too long. Last week we asked ourselves, why are we still in this foul place? Have you, Galveston Empire, kept us here? Or have we been imprisoned by our own fear of you, our own terror? So we're moving on. You won't stop us. Nothing stops the dead. In case you never noticed. LOL. And in case you're still plotting a future mine, you better stop that right now.

Next full moon we're swimming to the fen. We're armed with telepathic maledictions, and you'll have no defense against them. The veil between the worlds will be torn away. The future hides in electrical pulses along the mycelium highways. There, orchids will grow teeth, and water snakes will feed you to their young. Bacteria will digest your crane lifts, your dragline excavators, your stackers and crushers. Leeches will become engorged on your overfed bodies.

The future is a refuge, hiding. Each being is a cell of the fen-body.

FYI, the fen belongs to itself. Like us, it protects its own. It is a force like no other. It has no mercy.

Seeds

The seeds of the orchid, fine as dust, travel in the wind, attach themselves to animals, and are dispersed far and wide through forest, taiga and fen (Frost et al. 2032, 257).

Additionally, they can be ingested, along with the leaves and petals, either for the purposes of dissemination or as medicine. Knowledge from folk and oral traditions claims they have life-giving properties, and some current research bears this out, although it is cautioned that the therapy must be carried out only under the supervision of a doctor or other medical professional (Salvia, Jessie A. 1997, 23).

References

Frost, Kent et al. 2032. *Travels of the Seed.* Chambers & Ingram.
Salvia, Jessie A. 1997. "Various Uses of the Wild Orchid." *Orchidaceae Botanica* 15(10): 12-38.

Orchid Love

Mam and Irene are in the garden, sitting on the uncomfortable aluminum chairs. Their bare feet are in the grass, their faces to the sun.

"Orchid, murri shey," says my mother when she sees me. "Come sit with us."

But I'm restless; I can't stay still. Instead I go down to the stream, following till it widens into the marsh with its islets of cotton grass and moss. I smell the vanilla-scented orchids before I see them, the last orchids of the year.

So much of fen life feels ephemeral, but the fen is especially unsteady now. The ground has shifted, but the islets are always unstable, settling into roving patterns. Some cling to the shore, others shiver on the marsh currents. This is to be expected: you can't return twice to the same body of water. Threads gather, ephemera congeals, but never in precisely the same way. The fen is preparing itself for the panni raklies in whatever form they'll take.

Around the bend among the islets, Jack and Queenie are half-submerged, entwined. Queenie is grey and spent, nearly transparent. Hair dry as straw over her bent shoulders, falling over her boneless fingers. The exhaustion of sacrifice, known to so many women. But Jack — what horror or wonder is this? I'm flooded with dread, love, desire for him. Jack, lacy as burning mist, fading in and out, shifts on the unsteady islet. Hollow and dark, he is alive with untold stories, small burrowing creatures, tendrils and roots. Jack, green man of the fen, turns his face to show me his unreadable eyes.

Even though she can barely lift her hand, Queenie reaches for the flowers. She's feeding him orchids.

Who, what I am, what I'm part of, what I'm descended from — beauty, misery, tradition — grounds my feet at the shore. As do the orchids, their fungus, and the pollinators in the fen, we Romanies seek balance in everything: sky-earth, death-life, leaf-sign, the pure against the defiled. I honor the joining of the fen life — its rhizomes, tendrils, fins and wings — to the body and beating core of Jack in Queenie's healing hands. I honor the purity taught to me by my mother, shaped in my core by my desire, always shining, shining.

At night in our unbroken bed I turn to him. I sink into his new skin, fleshy as petals, his feet like roots, toes feeling for mine, his legs wrapping round my stem. We're swaddled by leaves. We slip so easily from one into the other. I fall into the open lip and slide, slide.

Acknowledgments

Deepest thanks to my initial guide and mentor, Daisuke Shen (author of *Vague Predictions & Prophecies*); to Eric Mills; to my parents, whose lives and stories inspired so much of this book; and to editor extraordinaire Selena Middleton, who supported and advised me during the development of the manuscript, generously infusing this story with her insight and wisdom.

About the Author

Lynn Hutchinson Lee was first place winner of the 2022 Joy Kogawa Award for Fiction. Her writing is published in *Room, Weird Horror, Fusion Fragment, Northern Nights* (Undertow Publications), Prairie Fire's *50 Over 50*, Guernica's *This Will Only Take a Minute* (winning the Editor's Choice Award), and elsewhere. She is co-editor of *Through the Portal: Stories From a Hopeful Dystopia* (Exile Editions). Following her novella, her novel *Nightshade*, shortlisted for the 2023 Guernica Prize, will be released by Assembly Press in 2025. She lives in Toronto with her partner. Visit her at www.lynnhutchinsonlee.ca.

YOU MAY ALSO LIKE

these Canadian titles from Stelliform Press!

Winner of the 2023 Ursula K. Le Guin Prize for Fiction, Rebecca Campbell's Arboreality is a novella in short stories about what it takes to survive and thrive in a climate changed world.

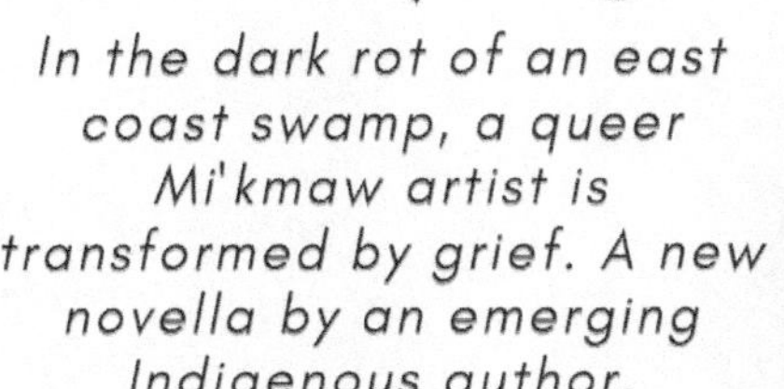

In the dark rot of an east coast swamp, a queer Mi'kmaw artist is transformed by grief. A new novella by an emerging Indigenous author.

**Earth-focused fiction. Stellar stories.
Stelliform.press.**

Stelliform Press is shaping conversations about our climate changed world and our place within it. We invite you to join the conversation by leaving a comment or review on your favorite social media platform. Find us on the web at www.stelliform.press and on Mastodon, Bluesky, Instagram, Facebook, Threads @StelliformPress.